Father Jacko's
GOZO STORIES

Martyn Offord

First published in 2018 by
FARAXA
www.faraxabooks.com / www.faraxapublishing.com
info@faraxapublishing.com

Fr Jacko's Gozo Stories
© 2018 Martyn Offord

Interior design / pagesetting by Faraxa Publishing

Front cover design by Ryan Galea and Philip Taliana

Editing & Proofreading by *Editizing*.com
and Ramona Vassallo

ISBN 978-99957-48-86-9

Printed in UK.

Dedication

*To Uncle Herb,
who introduced us to Gozo and who could
have been in some of these stories.*

Contents

Introduction

Gozo as I first knew it was a softly sunny island of donkey carts, lira, little traffic and multitudes of priests who were very visible, often reprimanding tourists for wearing their bikini tops away from the beach. Tourism was in its infancy, the foundations of a few apartment blocks were being laid and it was all proceeding in a very leisurely way. This was when most of these stories were written. I can't remember exactly when, but probably in the late eighties or early nineties; certainly, well before the euro and Wi-Fi hotspots.

Almost everything in these stories is true, or nearly true, or could have been true. I saw people who might have been the people I wrote about and by their gesturing and shrugging they may have been having the conversations I imagined for them. The warmth of the sunshine, the gentle pace of life, the kindness, charm and good humour are facts and remain facts.

Of course, many of the characters would have only spoken English as a second language and I have had to make them more fluent in that language than they probably would have been or would have even cared to be. Sometimes I used real place names, but where I haven't, readers who know the island will instantly recognise them.

I had forgotten about the stories and discovered them when clearing out our garage 20-30 years after their composition. Since the stories were written over a long period I reworked them a little to gain some continuity. Time, I'm afraid, is sometimes treated rather laxly, but part of Gozo's appeal for me has always been its rather casual attitude towards time. The story, 'Stardom', was added in 2017.

Gozo is made of hard unyielding rock, of seas that have dried up in the Mediterranean heat. Though currents swirl around the island and storms pound its edges, eventually collapsing the great Azure Window, its essence and character have not changed. I'm always delighted when I arrive to find that, despite the new ferry terminal and the flowers on the roundabouts, the same pot-holes are still there, the same sun that shines, the same charm, the same island.

Martyn Offord

Like A Flamingo

It was like a shard of ice splitting the right-hand side of his face and searing through into his ear. Gingerly feeling his tooth with the tip of his tongue, Barry realised that a filling had come out into his ice-cream cone and he was off on his holidays next week. At least he'd booked his leave. Tomorrow he'd go to his usual travel agent and find a cheap deal for a late booking. As long as he avoided the school holidays by a day or two they could always find room on a flight for one. But now he would need to get to a dentist first.

He ambled along the promenade of the small seaside town, carefully licking his cone and allowing it to melt in the pouch of his left cheek. It was an unusually hot day for late March and it had brought Sunday afternoon trippers to the coast for a trailer of summer. The little shops, despite a lack of stock, were open, with a few of last summer's sun hats and footballs dangling in nets beside the doorways. The revolving racks of bleached postcards were virtually empty but had been put out onto the pavements nevertheless.

Barry wore his shorts and an old pair of scuffed plimsolls. His body was smooth and always bronzed but at fifty-five his chest now hung slack and small with a tight paunch bulging at his belt. His legs were brown and strong but a tell-tale network of varicose veins welted under the skin of his left calf. Over his back he carried a small haversack which contained a towel and bathing costume, a woollen shirt, a cheap thriller and some sun-lotion.

Leaving the trippers behind, he clambered through a dyke and into the lee of the sea wall, trudging a mile or so along a baked and rutted mud path which edged the salt marshes to his right. A cool March wind blew off the sea and sifted through the reeds, rattling them and sending light green creases folding like waves inland. He walked on automatically, following the route he always took on Sunday afternoons, his head bowed and his tongue cautiously probing the cleft in his tooth. He passed the rusting shell of an old car upturned in the ditch, a landmark that had been there as long as he could remember and, as usual, he wondered who had taken the trouble to bring an old car all this way along an impossible path just to dump it in a ditch. A few yards further on, he mounted the sea wall and paused to put on his shirt as a snappy easterly wind breezed in from the sea. He stumbled a short way through some low dunes, the sand filling his shoes and the tough flails of marram grass whipping his shins, until he came down to the firmer sand at the sea's edge. Dodging the water which flowed in and slunk back, he strode on into the afternoon sun, over the flotsam of tangled ropes and plastic cartons which were strewn along the tide line.

He would have to phone the dentist and make an emergency appointment. It was a nuisance. His mother and Albert would overhear him on the phone and question him and find out that he had booked his holiday without telling them again.

"I'm going to see about a flat, I might just retire and go and live there," he'd mumble in his low East Anglian drawl, not looking at their piercing, mocking eyes.

"You've been saying that for ten years," his mother would sing-song and cackle. "You'll never leave home, boy."

He thought of them now: Albert, his mother's live-in partner who had materialised in the house sometime during Barry's teens, asleep on the settee; his mother, her legs in grey support stockings, her hearing-aid switched off spitefully to make everyone shout, watching Sunday afternoon soaps. The curtains would be closed and not a hint of the warm spring light would penetrate that room. He had cooked their Sunday lunch and left the washing up. But it would still be there when he returned. Albert hadn't worked in years and his mother, though she could walk perfectly well when it suited her, invariably proclaimed herself an invalid when there were chores to be done. So, he, the only son, had lived there all his life supporting and slaving for them both.

Five years ago, Barry had paused by the lychgate of his local church. A red line reached rather hopelessly towards the target amount needed for a new church roof. Barry took his building society pass book from his pocket and stared almost in hatred at the zeros that were accumulating, the interest amounts added; the hours of work and overtime clocked, the life totted up in columns credited in noughts. He wrote a cheque, went in the church and shoved it in a collection box. A few days later a shy young man with steamed up glasses and drooping eyes had appeared at the door, introducing himself as the church treasurer and asked for a word. Barry was conscious of pricked up ears in the darkened, front room where Albert and his mother had been waiting for him to get home from work to make their tea. He ushered the visitor into the kitchen where they sat awkwardly on opposite sides of the kitchen table, the young man fumbling in his brief case. Of course, the mother had now shuffled into the kitchen in her elasticated stockings with her hearing aid switched on and had begun to clatter about at the sink, in a poor pretence of washing up.

The young man passed the crumpled cheque across the table. "I think you may have made this out wrongly," he stammered.

"Nope, I never," Barry grunted and opened his building society pass book and showed him the latest page. The young man's eyes widened and he exhaled rather loudly.

"I work hard," Barry mumbled on. "Do overtime. General repairs. Odd jobs. Money just gathers. Nothin' to spend it on. Church might as well have some of it."

The young man now clearly felt more in his element. "You should be investing this in property or something more profitable than a building society account. Make the money earn you an income. Retire."

"I was thinkin' about that," Barry retorted, almost believing that he was. "I was thinkin' of getting a place abroad. In the sun."

The old woman had now dropped her pretence at the sink.

"In the sun!" she guffawed. "That's what he always says. He ain't ever gonna buy no place in the sun. An' he won't be spending none of it on us, that's for certain." And with one last cackle she shuffled out of the kitchen.

Now, on the first Sunday of summertime and with the extra hour of daylight, Barry rambled on in the slanting sun to where a small muddy rivulet flowed out and a long spit of sand stuck out into the sea. He removed his plimsolls and savoured the cold slurp of his feet as he trod the soft ripples of mud. Wading purposefully inland through the dunes, he dropped his haversack and rummaged amongst the grass and sand. He disinterred an old polythene sheet and some sticks and quickly erected a makeshift wind-break between himself and the sea. Down in the shelter from the wind was the perfect suntrap. He removed his shirt and surveyed the scene. A mile of salt-marsh bisected by deep muddy gullies separated him from the road and two miles of coarse white beach lay between him and the town.

The bright sun slipping in the sky exacerbated the huge glaring flatness of it all, and in the solitude Barry slipped out of his shorts and lay down to enjoy the warmth on his body and read his novel.

Sometime after four o'clock he stretched and stood up. The sprawling loneliness was cooler now. Some straggly clouds lay along the western horizon and behind them the sun, its yellow like an old, cold scorch mark in the sky. Barry shivered, but before he could bend to retrieve his clothes a flap of pink, white and black at the end of the sand-spit caught his eyes. He stared in disbelief. A flamingo strutted imperiously on pink wire legs, pausing to scoop in the edge of the tide with its hooked Roman beak. He had read about it in the local paper. It had escaped from a wild-life park a week or so ago and had been sighted several times stalking the coastal estuaries. A 'gregarious bird, a native of North Africa,' the paper had said, doomed to a lonely summer and probable death in the cold North Sea gloom of the next east coast winter. Fascinated, Barry watched it, standing alone, alone and exposed like him, surveying the grey flat waters then dipping its proud head and pecking the shallows, unaware of being watched in the vast ranging loneliness.

Then there was a movement, a gasp and a giggle behind him. Barry found his naked self the object of wide-eyed astonishment as two small girls suddenly hove out of the dunes not ten feet from him.

"Thee the thamingtho, thook! Thout on the thit!" Barry urged them, pointing excitedly out to where the bird strode in its splendour. But his missing filling siphoned the air through the gaping hole in his tooth in an indecipherable lisp and all the children registered was a naked man standing before them, waving his arms and hissing gibberish at them.

They screamed and ran, gesturing shrilly as their parents gathered them up in alarm and glared in horror at the stark ravisher of their daughters who stood in dark silhouette on the dunes. Barry clutched a towel in front of him as the sun seeped into the marshes behind him. He watched the angry and violated little family group hurrying along the beach.

It was time to leave this place which Barry knew: the world of families, this beach, his mother and Albert, this country, this life. The flamingo, disturbed by the rumpus, rose into the sky and, with a flap of its black-edged wings, wheeled on some instinct and flew into the sun, its long neck stretched before it and the thin wire legs trailing behind.

Two days later Barry gazed at the travel brochures in the dentist's waiting room. He blinked at the surreal yellows and blues, the breaking surf on rocks and golden coloured flat roofed houses, the bougainvillea, the oleander along the paths. One more week until the high church spire above the harbour bobbed into sight and Barry disembarked in Gozo for the first time.

That Famous
Top B Flat

To the onlookers, sprawled in the shade of the mulberry trees, Father Jacko might have been kissing the hibiscus flower. Actually, it was because he was so short-sighted. The plant grew in an untidy patch of parched earth beside the broad marble steps that led up to the Basilica. The shabby old priest was peering through the Coca-Cola bottled bottoms of his glasses at the stamen that seemed to lick out at him like a dry pink tongue. "The hibiscus flowers in the fresh dew of the morning, blooms through the heat of the day and dies at night," he intoned to himself; a sermon he knew Father Thomas would never allow him to preach. "But next day new flowers will bloom, perpetually resurrected like the Christ," he resumed to his imaginary congregation. A sharp voice called his name. Still bending, he looked round, squinting against the afternoon sun that dazzled yellow on the sandstone buildings. Hazily, through his myopic eyes, he saw the brown and navy blur of the village men slumped in the shade outside Joe Farrugia's bar across the square. The voice came again, angrier this time. Father Jacko straightened his stiff back and lumbered up the steps and across the terrace to where Father Thomas stood beneath the veined marble arch of the doorway.

"Where have you been? And I thought I told you to wear something more respectable," the senior priest hissed, his superior Maltese eyes looking despairingly down at the broken sandals that seemed soldered onto the Gozitan's broad, bare peasant feet. The soutane hanging shapelessly from Jacko's thin shoulders was stained with tar from the beaches as well as fig juice and green slime from the crushed fennel and clover he sprawled amongst during his rambles on the hillsides. As a gesture to respectability, Jacko brushed some of the dust from his sleeves. Father Thomas looked prayerfully into the searing light of heaven, huffed and sighed.

"We only have centenaries every hundred years, you know," he muttered, turning and leading his subordinate into the great church. Father Jacko reflected upon this for a moment and followed; half listening to the salvo of instructions he was being given. He blinked in the cool aqueous light inside.

He never felt comfortable in here. Jacko wouldn't admit it, but he didn't like the smooth pink plaster

Christs that reared up on either side of the portico as he entered, with their macabre thorns and ropes, their whip welts and trickles of blood. He loved the cool split marble columns though, echoing each other's pink filament patterns on the pillars of the nave, because they were natural and had simply been opened out by the masons to reveal their glory. The dense gloomy paintings and gilded ornamentation that crowded every surface of the walls and ceiling, however, suffocated him.

"Just make sure you stay within hearing and do as you're told," Father Thomas was snapping beneath his breath. "Eddie will help you."

Eddie, the general dogsbody, crept out from the shadow of a side chapel looking as if his ministrations to the church were some awful penance for some forgotten sin. He had put on an ill-fitting suit for the occasion and squirmed in the high collar that rose to collide with his thick black wedges of sideburns. His huge flat hands hung limp several inches below his frayed shirt cuffs.

The famous English orchestra was assembling in the transept beneath the giant dome. Fair-haired young men with pink faces were unpacking violins from cases whilst lady cello players boomed to each other and tightened their strings. A flute fluttered, its sound reverberating like a giggle down the high nave. Father Thomas approached the conductor and nodded deferentially as the man motioned hither and thither indicating all that needed altering. Fingers were clicked and orders rattled, while Jacko and Eddie were dispatched into vestries and closets, scampering down aisles doing this and that of what was wrong and needed fixing. They pushed the rostrum a foot to the left and back again; they tried to unfold metal music stands and bent them; Jacko was sent off to fetch a jug of water, forgot what he was after and came back with a vase. Finally, in despair, Father Thomas commanded them to straighten the rows of chairs, a job which he deemed might be within the scope of their organisational capabilities.

As the afternoon sun slanted in through the high stained-glass, the famous Italian soprano made her entrance, billowing through the percolated coloured light, ignoring bowing priests and advancing with outstretched hand towards the famous conductor. For a moment the two famous musicians saluted each other extravagantly. He indicated to her the split marble columns, the ornate dome and the lofty ceiling with its smothering of saints, martyrdoms and miracles depicted by local artists. She surveyed it all imperiously and gestured airily with her hands, each gesture culminating in the right hand returning to the famous bosom which swam out from under her light summer coat.

It was announced that she was going to test the acoustics.

The conductor helped her remove her jacket and Father Jacko, from the bottom rung of the ladder he was holding for Eddie, blinked the filminess from his eyes as the cleavage was unveiled, its dark impenetrable rift awakening thoughts of the deep ravine which sank lushly down to Mgarr ix-Xini.

The strings stopped scraping; the oboes and clarinets fell silent. Jacko and Eddie were hastily driven to the obscurity at the rear of the building. Two or three urchins in bare feet were peeping through the doorway, the harsh light on the backs of their heads, and a couple of old men who had shuffled across the square crept in uncertainly. They held their caps awkwardly before them and stood on their buckled old legs, their dusty toes turned inward. All was silent and expectant. Jacko invited the locals further in to witness the sacrament of the acoustics that were about to be tested, but Father Thomas quickly bustled down the aisle and shooed them out, permitting Jacko and Eddie to remain only on the condition that they remained quiet.

The great fathomless bosom heaved and the lips seemed to curl back and wrap themselves around the teeth. The scale arose from deep within the diaphragm, on a spiralling thermal of sound to the dome, revolved around the galleries, swelled out and filled the nave and lifted to the roof, to the ears of the saints and martyrs who, for a hundred years, had heard nothing except the dull chanting of priests and the thin psalms of peasant congregations. Then the singer climaxed on her famous Top B flat and smiled as the echo returned fully to her.

There was a wondrous hush and then, from high in the shadows above, where the legs of St Stephen, stoned and bleeding curved down from the arch of the roof, a cricket started chirruping. It chirruped throughout the rehearsal, its voice a regular shrill squeak like the turning of an unoiled bicycle wheel. There were, of course, many jokes about its pitch and key and its staccato four-four-time. Even the famous soprano condescended to remark upon its fortissimo. But as the rehearsal ended the famous conductor took Father Thomas by the sleeve of his soutane and snapped between his teeth, "Madam is not pleased. The creature must be gone by tonight. It ruined her cadenza meno mosso."

And so it was, after the Basilica had been cleared and prepared for the centenary concert, and after the door had been shut on the villagers who stared from the tables outside the bars at the pink English people clambering into their air-conditioned coach, that Father Jacko began his nervous climb up the uneven steps of the dark, spiral staircase that led to the narrow gallery which ran around just below the roof. In all his years as an assistant priest he had never been up here. His hands fumbled on the rough wooden rail and his toes stubbed against the stone steps. The air seemed thick and fetid in the narrow stairwell and he kept pausing to gain breath. There were unfamiliar smells of damp or bats or of mildew. Eventually he crawled through a low doorway and out onto a precariously narrow parapet that ran the length of the nave.

Father Thomas had virtually seized him and thrust him through the concealed wooden doorway behind the Statue of the Annunciation. "Make sure you get rid of the cricket," he had yelled hysterically, and shut the door on him.

Poor Father Jacko knew that no one as short-sighted as he was could ever find a cricket. Anyway, it had stopped now. He peered through his thick lenses at the narrow ledge of stone he was supposed to crawl along. He hadn't realised before that someone could actually make their way along here. Presumably the original masons and artists had used it to support their scaffolding. Kneeling in the thick dust, he put his hand carefully on the highly ornate gilded rail that one admired with all the other gilded fretwork from below. Then, slowly and laboriously, he began to manoeuvre his way along. Once he looked down to the marble slabs and tombstones below, swallowed hard and resolved to look up instead each time he paused from his cautious groping.

The frescos were huge and bland. Mellow, reddish light suffused the dim interior of the Basilica yet failed to soften the garish primary colours and the sickly plastic complexions of the heavenly assembly. He had heard that the ceiling had been painted a hundred years ago by a local peasant artist whose family still lived in the village. He imagined this painter, cramped and complaining, inevitably unpaid, reluctantly fulfilling the priests' commission. At this close range Jacko could see there was no commitment or spiritual investment; the figures were crude and primitive and the artist had been careless and shoddy with detail. The faces weren't local, browned by the island sun and wind, but blond and insipid with a north European pallor and expressionless. Fragments of paintings that were invisible from below hadn't even been finished. The bleeding legs of the martyred St Stephen had no feet, for instance. What appeared from the floor to be grazes on Cain's knuckles was in fact merely the paint flaking away.

After what seemed like hours, Jacko had succeeded in inching his way the length of the gallery to a point parallel to the conductor's rostrum. It was here, on the ledge itself, with a gasp of pleasure and surprise that Jacko found a perfect miniature painting, with the most delicate of brushwork and with every detail lovingly finished. Gently he brushed the dust away and stretched himself full length along the overhang so he could inspect it closely with his tired, watery eyes. God was creating the universe. He had an uncannily familiar Gozitan peasant face, strong-featured, brown and angular. With His paintbrush

He was bringing into existence the vine terraces and the lemon groves around the village, the fishing boats with their ancient eyes, the lace bobbins and the wine flagons, the stone walls with the vetch tumbling out of the cracks.

Jacko giggled with delight at the defiance and irreverence of it all. The artist had presented himself as God the creator – the greatest of blasphemies, which was why the tiny mural had been so carefully hidden. In the corner, in a script as fine as a coiled hair, was written: "This is what I can really create. Joseph Farrugia." Jacko chuckled at the realisation that the features of God were distinctly those of the Farrugias who still formed a large part of the local populace. In fact, a Joseph Farrugia owned the bar shaded by the mulberry trees across the square. The splendid, gilded concert about to be enacted below was actually celebrating the centenary of Joseph Farrugia's cocked snook at the church establishment and Father Thomas's illustrious forebears. Frustrated with the effete idealised figures he had been instructed to paint to the glory of God, the original artist, with typical Farrugia stubbornness and anti-clericalism, had vented his frustration in this tiny, perfect square of genius, visible only on this ledge. And Jacko had been invited into this secret and impious peasant joke which the famous soprano had unwittingly revealed with her laudatory Top B Flat.

He must have been enjoying the joke for some time, because suddenly the great door swung open, pouring an ochre evening light into the aisle, and in marched Father Thomas accompanied by the Monsignor from Malta, both in their best clerical suits. They were followed by the orchestra and the famous conductor, all in evening dress. Jacko gulped and flattened himself against the ledge. He realised he couldn't turn around to crawl back again and there was nothing for it now but to wedge himself against the wall and hide in the deepening shadows.

By twisting his neck round he could watch the church filling up. The humbler members of the community were first, edging nervously into the chairs at the back. The dim evening light was restful on Jacko's strained eyes and he could identify the audience members as they arrived. There was his brother, Francis, the estate agent, careful to acknowledge the dignitaries, but hesitating at the second row and retreating to the further side of the nave. Eddie loitered near a pillar, furtive, anxious, guilty looking. Several Maltese visitors marched forward and re-arranged the chairs to their liking. The front rows remained reserved for local dignitaries who would make their entrances late so as to be seen by as many of their inferiors as possible. He saw Father Thomas glaring around angrily, presumably looking for him, and eventually marshalling Eddie and one or two others whom he extracted from the shadows, to the fore of the nave with extra chairs to plonk right in the front for the clergy. The last was a tactical move undertaken when the secular dignitaries were installed so as to ensure that the spiritual estate took precedence.

The orchestra was tuned and there was the silence that anticipated the mounting of the rostrum by the famous conductor. Instead there was a clicking of high heels and in minced the bank manager, his wife in a glinting, silver dress dripping with jewellery and a lace shawl draped across her shoulders; he in a cool blue suit, smiling easily and acknowledging acquaintances with a wave of his emerald ringed finger. From his aerial vantage point Jacko could see the scowl of the conductor who had taken a step into the public view and then had had to retire until the late arrivals condescended to relinquish the limelight.

The first half of the centenary concert ended in enthusiastic applause. After the conductor had ensured the bank manager and his wife were in position, he re-entered for the second part, took his baton and then fetched the famous soprano to her position on the chancel steps. Her voluminous dress sparkled and billowed like a marquee from its highest anchor point three-quarters of the way down her bosom, to trail out around her feet. Out of respect for the church a light shawl hung across her shoulders but, nevertheless, from his aerie directly above her

Jacko found himself forced to gape down into the great spilling pillows of her breasts.

By now he was feeling rather cramped. His elbow was sore and his wrist was bent backwards from supporting his head. Moreover, sharp pains were shooting down his outside leg which, for over an hour now, had been propping his body tight against the wall.

The orchestra raced to a climax and stopped as the soprano's voice hesitated and trembled on the low vibrato which commenced the long-awaited cadenza meno mosso. The whole congregation seemed to be teetering on her breath, anticipating the famous moment when the miracle of sound would awaken the shadows and roll ineffably around the great dome. The great bosom expanded and slowly the voice ascended, exploring the shades of the notes, dipping and sliding, but climbing, climbing relentlessly towards that famous Top B Flat for which the audience was waiting. However as it pitched awesomely to the Top B Flat, instead of stopping and triumphing at its peak, it rose higher and higher into a realm where all notions of music were left beneath it, transcending all acoustics and mutating into a scream of utter terror. For as she had lifted her eyes to match her splendid crescendo, Jacko, in trying to adjust his position had suddenly rolled to the edge of the parapet, his soutane had become caught around the railing as he grabbed at it, and a brown bandy leg naked to the thighs, had swung down out of the shadows above her. Audience, orchestra, famous conductor, famous soprano, the Monsignor and Father Thomas watched mesmerised as one old sandal detached itself from a hanging foot. It seemed to linger in mid-air and then dived like a swallow to land among the cymbals and bounce across the timpani. With all the noise the cricket started again.

The hibiscus flower had closed its petals and died until tomorrow. Father Jacko sat in the dimmest corner of Joseph Farrugia's bar sipping at a glass of dark bitter wine and playing cards. The other players pressed closely around him wrapping him in a comfortable swathe of nicotine and beery breath to conceal him from the vengeful Father Thomas who was glaring furiously through the doorway. Farrugia's strong brown angular features grinned across the counter. He had inherited his ancestor's stubborn pleasure in thwarting the clerical establishment.

"He didn't see you," he announced at last. "But I hope you've got a good story for when he does catch you – it had better not be the truth, mind you. They never like the truth."

Snorkelling for a Cross

Father Jacko strode round the stony cliff path because he had seen blue-white smoke puffing up against the sky and wondered who had a fire. The sun clouted the zinc sea and he had to shield his weak eyes. It was Marc. He was burning an old tamarisk tree that had been dried, bent and twisted by years of wind and heat until finally it had slumped over, its shallow roots raised in a mockery of gnarled fingers. The wood crackled savagely, popping and spitting hot bark. Jacko helped Marc load on last year's dried thistles which had been scythed and raked into a heap. Thick choking smoke seeped out until a flame licked up and the thistles blazed, charred and collapsed inward.

The two men shared a hunk of bread and a huge sweet tomato, lamenting the proliferation of thistles since the locals had stopped keeping donkeys and goats. The smoke stung Jacko's eyes. He removed his glasses and looking for something to dab his aching eyes with resorted to the sleeve of his soutane. Marc saw the pink edges of the lids and the watery feeble squint and felt remorse.

"My wife has needed me to help with Margaret, so I've not got down to Mass," he lied.

Without answering, Jacko replaced his spectacles. The sorrow in his tired, stinging eyes seemed magnified through the thick lenses.

"But I will be there for Good Friday," Marc added guiltily and untruthfully.

It was not a real lie because both men tacitly understood that it would not be so. The lie was only in the spoken sound which was grunted into the fire and dispersed by wood-smoke; it was not in the meaning. Nevertheless, it was with a heavy sadness that Jacko continued on round the cliff path. A birdless silence hung tensely in the air. Only the drone of the bees among the clover accompanied him. The path skirted an outcrop of jagged grey rock and wound down to a thick stand of bamboo where a tiny stream oozed through the shingle and grasses to the sea below. Here the priest paused in the cool lattice-worked light beneath a fig tree and stared back up to where the meagre plume of smoke still drifted above the ridge.

He was disappointed that Marc had lied to him but understood his anger and disbelief. For months his young daughter had been sick. Whatever the medicine or the church had offered had failed, so

Marc had rejected the latter and couldn't afford the former. Because of his outspokenness on religious matters the people felt uneasy about patronising the little shop his wife ran, so that was failing too, hence the lack of ready money and inability to meet the medical bills.

Distracted by these thoughts and with his dim vision mistaking the way, Jacko discovered that the path had petered out amongst the rocks and scree that over the years had eased their way from the cliffs above and slid down to the margins of the sea. Contorting his face and narrowing his eyes to gauge a route ahead, he clambered through sharp-edged boulders until he stood on a great slanting slab of stone which sloped like a giant piece of paving to the edge of the water. Standing there, sheltered from the wind, he felt the springtime sun hot on the rocks and on the baldness of his head. From the pocket of his dusty soutane he took a rather grimy beret and put it on.

Sometimes the sea would ripple to his feet and flop back gently. Then if a breeze found its way through the tumbled boulders of the headland, it spread the water flat so it lay supine, eerily silent and still. Jacko could then see down into the water as far as his short-sightedness would allow, to where the edge of the slab made a vertical drop. Perhaps it was because his shoulders were hunched and his head bowed low with the burden of Marc's lie to him, or because the sun reeled across the water and dazed his eyes; or perhaps it was because his vision melted in and out of focus as it strained down into the aqueous depths, but as the water sprawled at his feet, Jacko was sure he saw the outline of a cross partly submerged in the sand of the sea-bed. Then the image became ruffled and dispersed as the surface water slurped upwards again and slapped among the rocks. He waited as it subsided and there again, as a honeyed spar of sunlight lit the sea-bed, he saw the cross, rippling and dilating in the water. Though the sand trickled over it and though it leaned to one side like a tired man on his elbow, Jacko saw its rough black grain and splintered edges before the sea heaved from its torpor and the cross and the rocks of the sea-bed fragmented and wafted away again. Jacko removed his glasses and stared down, but without them the stone at his feet and the veined rocks around him, the sky and the cliffs above, all swam in an underwater translucence.

Every day after that, throughout the week leading up to Easter, Father Jacko scrambled and groped his way down through the thistles and across the debris to the great slanting pavement of rock. But now the sea always scurried in and broke at his feet, or the surface ebbed and swelled, or the sun clouded over, so that Jacko wondered if in his short-sightedness and in Marc's lying, he had only imagined and hoped for a cross that was not there. He just needed to be certain of that vision to give him the strength to confront the sadness of Marc's unbelief. As he stood there on Good Friday afternoon after a mass from which Marc had inevitably been absent, he wondered if he too, like Marc, should dismiss the cross as the mere playfulness of sunlight, water and myopia. In his vacant state he picked up an old discarded piece of rag left idly on the rock to wipe his glasses. He cleaned the lenses thoughtfully while the sea and rocks blurred into golden, aching, sun-filled fuzz.

Barry, who was treading water rather shyly behind a rock, watched the priest wiping his spectacles with his underpants. After a couple of holidays wandering alone, exploring the island, he had discovered this remote sun-trap this morning, slipped out of his clothes and spread himself unselfconsciously on the rock to sunbathe. Every so often when he felt hot, he slipped naked into the cold springtime sea for a bit of snorkelling. Ten minutes of swimming was as much as he could comfortably bear and he had been waiting for a quarter of an hour for the priest to go away so he could emerge, jump up and down a few times to warm himself and then dry off with his towel. He suspected that priests on this island might be rather intolerant of nude activities but circumstances had now reached crisis point. Faced with a choice between hyperthermia and hell-fire, he decided upon the warmer.

Keeping his head low and making as little disturbance as possible, he glided carefully towards the shore. He was breathing quietly through his snorkel with his mask half submerged. Through it the priest was hugely magnified as he materialised into view each time Barry rose on the swell. Eventually, when he was about to rise fully exposed from the waves, the priest seemed to notice him. His eyes blinked several times, presumably in shock, and his whole face screwed up into what appeared to be disgust.

In fact, staring into the sea, Jacko had become aware of a dark shape with a vertical stick protruding bobbing towards him. Only when the form had groped among the rocks, loomed up dripping out of the water and Jacko had blinked several times, did the blurred shape then become distinguishable as a man.

Barry, half crouching as if winded, covered his shame with his mask, then, realising that the mask magnified his shame, quickly snatched it away and thrust his snorkel between his legs instead. That move was clearly rather awkward also and he continued to juggle with his equipment whilst he sidled around the edge of the rock platform, mumbling apologies and reaching out hopefully for the underpants which Jacko was still clutching. All this was lost on the priest of course, who, replacing his glasses, found they had steamed up. All he could see was the furry outline of a crouching bear-like creature holding out its paw in a begging attitude and mumbling something in English about being sorry and having a dip.

Barry on the other hand, revolving around the rock at as modest an angle as he could achieve, couldn't understand why the priest was squinting at him, apparently indifferent to his nude state and muttering something about a cross down there.

Luckily the chill of the water had contracted Barry's genitals into a rather tight little wrinkled knot which even the compensation of the mask or the snorkel had failed to bring to Jacko's notice. At last Barry had his towel safely round him and Jacko wiped his glasses again and stuffed the rag into his pocket without realising what the item was, or to whom it belonged. Barry quickly decided to sacrifice his underpants in the interest of social ease and rapidly slipped into his unused bathing costume.

The Englishman's powers of conversation were rather unexercised but he was only required to listen. He spread himself languidly in the sunshine to warm up while the priest sat himself down, kicked off his sandals and told him about the cross he had seen at the foot of the shelf they were sitting on. Barry got stiffly to his feet and strolled to the edge to peer down.

"Of course, my eyesight is poor," Jacko was saying, "and I wouldn't be able to see something like that in the water normally, but for once, perhaps, despite my failings, I was allowed a vision."

Barry, ever pragmatic and unimpressed by visions, announced that the water was about fifteen feet deep and was moving too much to ever see anything.

"It was unusually still," Jacko argued. "Mysteriously still. Maybe in the eyes of my mind I saw it. Maybe the Lord just gave me a mental image." He sounded disappointed though, however hard he reasoned with himself.

"I ain't seen nothin' down there," Barry pronounced definitively. His blunt, East Anglian accent mind only registered crosses that were or crosses that were not. Crosses that were and yet were not evaded his stark logic. Barry didn't have eyes in his mind, only in his head.

"I've swum all around here," he drawled, "and there ain't no crosses I've seen." The intonation of his voice was final.

Jacko grimaced as if in pain. "It's a pity," he murmured at last. "It's an easy miracle, just to imagine a cross when I need one, but for me with my poor eyes, to see one which really *is* there when no one else can – then that really *is* a miracle. A miracle of the body, as well as of the imagination. I prefer physical miracles," he added wistfully. Something in his sad, inaudible supplication, penetrated through, even to Barry. "I'll have a look if you want," he mumbled.

Once the offer had been made there was no going back. He was hurried into his mask and snorkel, flippers were on his feet and he was urged back into the freezing water, but carefully so as not to disturb it. Barry caught his breath as the cold lunged at him, then, pausing for his body to adjust to the temperature; he swam to where Jacko was eagerly directing him to dive.

The priest knew no mercy. Despite his chattering teeth and threatened cramp Barry was ordered to dive and dive again. Eventually he found the great whispering and booming silence of being under the water less irksome than the jabbering tyranny of the excited priest, so he stayed under longer and longer. Wreathes and phalanxes of seaweed waved in the current and odd shaped stones glittered as stray shafts of sunlight pierced the water. A scurry of tiny fish brightly lit and coloured, with one instinct shot forward and retreated. Then he saw it – a dark wooden outline submerged in the sand, slightly askew with one arm dug deep and the other wedged upward between two boulders. Unwilling to lose sight of it, he took a deep breath through his snorkel. He heard it gutter with water as he dived. The pressure on his lungs became acute as he kicked his way down, but he couldn't reach it. Back at the surface he had lost his sense of direction and it took a moment to find Father Jacko. The priest was further off than he anticipated and was looking in the wrong direction. Barry shouted and waved. All Jacko could see was a flailing brown blob but he heard the cry and signalled back.

Down Barry went again kicking hard with his flippers. He was a strong swimmer and by grabbing hold of submerged rocks and forcing himself further, he was at last scrabbling about on the sea-bed with his fingers. Quickly, because his lungs rasped and his head was pounding, he brushed the sand away feeling the rough bulk with his hands. As he surfaced he almost screamed with pain. Salt water was syringing in his nose and behind his eyes and the sea detonated in his ears. Briny mucus scorched the back of his throat and then exploded in his nostrils. It was as if his lungs had burst. As Father Jacko hauled him ashore he felt the trickle of blood and mucus on his top lip and he seemed to be swimming in and out of consciousness. But Father Jacko didn't notice. He was almost dancing with curiosity. Impatient with Barry's swaying and choking, he was firing questions which ricocheted off Barry's numbed mind.

"You saw it? You saw it? You saw the cross?" he cried.

"It ain't no cross," Barry gasped. "It's an ole bit of a boat or a cart or summat."

"But it's cross-*shaped*," the priest insisted. "It's cross-*shaped*!"

Barry's dogged logic was being stretched beyond its normal limit.

"Well, yeah, it's cross-*shaped*," he conceded, "but it ain't no cross. I told you it's a bit of an old cart or of a boat."

There was a pause while Jacko's normally dim eyes seemed to sparkle with a glow which the dense glass of his lenses magnified into a heavenly fire.

"So, I have at last seen a cross," he cried in ecstasy. "A cross which floats ships or bears loads is a cross nevertheless."

Barry sniffed in answer and wiped the mucus from his nose with the back of his hand. He eyed Jacko's rapture rather doubtfully.

"Then you must come to Mass on Sunday. It will be in English for visitors, you see."

The conversation had taken a turn Barry hadn't followed and the prospect of lots of superstition, bell ringing and chanting made him shudder. He began to excuse himself.

"I'm Church of England. I don't believe in that sort of thing," he started, but Jacko cut in.

"And you don't believe that was a cross you saw either. *You* say a cart or a boat. *I* say a cross – and it's the same piece of wood. *You* had to get right close to see it. But *I* saw it with my feeble old eyes from right up here!"

Relishing his outburst, he scrambled away up the hillside leaving Barry gaping after him. From up the muddy footpath he could be heard crying out in triumph an unusual combination of texts: "Mine eyes have seen the glory of the coming of the Lord, now lettest thy servant depart in peace for mine eyes have seen thy salvation, glory, glory Hallelujah," and he waved his beret in the air.

From the pocket of Jacko's soutane Barry could see his underpants poking out.

The Missing Toe

Eddie was a handyman and often helped out at the church. He was in his forties, had great wedges of black sideburns and a trunk of matted greased hair which hung over his dark eyes. He lived with his mother in St Mary Street, across the narrow road from the hotel. During holiday weekends, however, they moved into the boat house of some relations and rented out their apartment.

As it was Easter weekend, crowds of young people from Malta had invaded the little harbour village. Late into the night they careered round the dusty streets in their cars, or revved up and down on their scooters, calling out to one another and playing their music loudly. A springtime storm had driven them indoors. Throughout the evening great-bellied clouds had swelled up in the sky and chilly squalls blew in from the sea. Shutters banged and loose cables cracked against the walls. The first rain fell in slow rhythmic drops, determined and penetrating. Then the pace quickened and suddenly a deluge swamped down, flushing the narrow streets and flowing in rivulets of mud down to the harbour. Overhead thunder rolled and crashed simultaneously with the lightning which vaulted in blue zigzag fractures across the night sky. Then, of course, the electric power failed.

The young folk who had rented Eddie's apartment didn't mind. Their music powered by batteries blared out and they shouted and laughed. In the hotel room opposite, Barry was unable to sleep so he opened his shutters and stared across at their balcony. He contemplated complaining but knew they wouldn't hear. Anyway, he had no idea how many there were, reckless and young, crammed into the tiny flat. He could see that they had pushed a bed right up against the balcony window and in an electric explosion of blue he saw a girl, her white underclothes illuminated in ultra-violet against her honey skin, kneeling on the bed as a youth crouched over her. Barry felt his decades of girl-less years and closed his shutters. He picked up some property brochures collected from a rather weary estate agent after having been driven around the island for most of the day looking at possible apartments. At the end of the excursion Barry had mumbled, "Oh, I dunno. Maybe it's too soon. Next year, p'haps." In the clammy darkness he fingered their glossy promise and, to thumping music and ripples of giggles, dilating shadows, apocalyptic thunder and savage pulses of lightning, Barry dozed off.

Dawn edged in grey and spectral. The air was strangely silent and limp as if the night had been wrung out like a dishcloth. Deep gullies rutted the road and the path was pitted with brown puddles. Barry was awakened from a fitful sleep by a gentle but urgent knocking coming from outside. Leaning out of his bed and pushing the shutters ajar he could hear a voice calling, "Eddie, Eddie. Wake up, Eddie."

By the time Barry was out of bed and peering over his balcony the sound had stopped and he heard the receding steps of Father Jacko, his old sandals splashing through the pools in the road and sending spatterings of mud over the frayed hem of his soutane. The Englishman watched the bowed, dishevelled form, the bald head the colour of the muddy water he trod through. At the foot of the street Jacko turned and mounted the broad marble steps to the church, wearily supporting himself, first on the statue of Jesus washing Peter's feet, and then in turn on each of the carved disciples that stood at regular intervals on the stone parapet. Each one, no less than Father Jacko, seemed huddled against the cold dawn light which was seeping damply in from the sea.

Barry was dozing off again when he heard a prolonged, coarse scraping on the wall opposite, followed by a metallic clatter and a slow, irregular, rubbery bouncing sound. Putting his eye to the shutters again, he saw the top of a ladder, convulsing as Father Jacko, slowly and in obvious terror, was climbing up. At every tentative step he paused and looked down, straining his eyes through his thick lenses, before looking up again and squinting at the balcony. His trembling hands clutched the ladder in panic and his knees were splayed out as he pressed himself against the rungs. After a painful few moments he grabbed the balcony rail, hauled himself up and tipped himself rather unceremoniously over the ironwork. Barry saw his glasses fall and land softly in the mud below.

Then Jacko started banging loudly on the shutters until they were prised open and a mop of black hair appeared as one of the youths looked out in alarm. Barry, now quite riveted as a spectator, could see the dark hair on his chest and the gold around his neck.

"Who the hell are you?" the youth demanded.

"Eddie, come quick, Eddie ... the storm ... timer ... re-setting," implored the priest.

"I'm not Eddie. Who's Eddie? My God, it's a priest!" the boy cried.

"Where's Eddie? I need Eddie."

"Eddie's not here, Father. I don't know any Eddie."

Inside a wrestle was obviously taking place as someone else struggled to open the shutters wider.

"Don't," the boy hissed back into the room. "It's a priest, for God's sake!"

But then the girl's head appeared, her hair tumbling down over her bare shoulders and a sheet clutched across her breast.

"Is that you, Mrs Vella?" Jacko asked, no doubt mistaking the tumble of glossy black hair for the old widow's black lace veil she wore to confession. "Where's Eddie?"

By now at least half a dozen voices were proclaiming the non-existence of Eddie and Barry could see dark shadows in the interior grabbing clothes and pulling sheets around themselves.

"Eddie sleeps in the far room," Jacko was saying. "Let me through, Mrs Vella, please. I need to see your son," he added, solemnly addressing the half-naked girl who sat on the bed and gently helped him through the balcony window, where he waded through the tangle of knickers and bed linen to the safety of the floor.

Barry watched the dim interior of the room billowing with activity. Doors seemed to be opening and closing and there was a scurrying of shirts and skirts, plumping of pillows and curtains, anxious voices and repressed giggling.

"Is it a raid?" he heard someone whisper. "By God, it's 1990!"

A few moments later Jacko, presumably satisfied that neither Eddie nor his mother were in residence, emerged from the street door. His old crumpled face, having seen everything, or nothing, betrayed nothing. He peered down into the mud, groped with his fingers and retrieved his glasses. Wiping them on his sleeve he blinked up at the ladder and carefully but simultaneously hazardously started moving it. Firstly, he pulled it from the wall and it stood poised, tottering vertically for a dangerous moment. Either it would fall forward and take the priest with it, or backwards and flatten him in the mud. But somehow, miraculously, Jacko lowered it and finding some sort of pivotal point under his arm, he staggered back towards the church, the backend swaying and crashing against the walls as he went.

By this time Barry was already pulling on some clothes so as to go and help the old priest. He had seen decorators going in and out of the church and presumably that was where the ladder was from. The prospect of Jacko trying to negotiate a twenty-foot ladder through the door rather alarmed him.

As Barry came out into the street he was just in time to see Jacko careen in a wide arc up the steps, bearing his twenty-foot ladder horizontally up a stairway fifteen feet wide. Jesus must have ducked but St. Peter received the brunt of the blow, swayed uncertainly, and then spiralled down into the mud with an ugly squelching noise.

Barry helped Jacko with the ladder and they then returned to the foot of the steps to inspect the damage. Luckily St Peter had had a soft landing in the mire of clay and silt which had accumulated against the parapet. Only part of the foot was broken where it had come away from its pedestal.

"Christ is supposed to be washing Peter's feet, not mending his broken leg," Jacko sighed.

Barry scratched his head and sniffed. "Any tools in the church ... trowel ... chisel ... mite o'cement? Do a bit of handiwork. Need to narrow the foot down a bit. Should be easy enough."

The first sunshine of the day glowed with a sense of purpose on Jacko's forehead. So, after reinstalling the statue, Barry was invited to reset the tape-recorder that played 'Ave Maria' on the hour and pealed out the bells that summoned the faithful to mass. The power cut in the night had upset the timing mechanism and this had occasioned the carnage of Father Jacko's search for Eddie that morning.

"You must come to Mass now," he instructed Barry who was washing a trowel and wiping it on his trousers. "It's in English, for the visitors. Father Thomas lets me take this one because not many people come."

Barry swallowed in alarm. "I don't know," he grunted, "all those bells an' candles an' stuff's beyond me. An' me trousers are dirty."

But Jacko wasn't listening and his excitement was mounting. "You won't be the only one," he exclaimed.

"There's another Englishman coming. I met him yesterday. He'd found a cross."

He squinted closely at St. Peter's foot which Jesus was again washing. "He's only got four toes!" he commented. "St. Peter's only got four toes. No matter. Jesus won't mind," and Jacko fairly bounced back up the steps as a salvo of shots from a huntsman in the hills ricocheted through the valley.

The shower in Barry's room was a crude affair. A rusted pipe, half screwed to the wall, led up to a drooping nozzle which expressed a rather lukewarm dribble as a spray. But Barry had never been one for luxuries and enjoyed the wash after the exertions of this Easter morning. On time he heard with some satisfaction the festive bells start off, at first with a grating and a choke and a slow slump of sound before the tape speeded up and the tower erupted into a peal of Easter joyousness. As the sound rattled across the flat roof tops, the clouds rolled back so that a cleansed and pristine sky lit the morning.

When the bells had stopped and the last straggler had entered the church, Barry ventured in. He regretted it immediately. Instead of the plain little statues of the disciples on the terrace outside, a pale watery virgin presided over a small piscine and a plaster Christ with a garish shredded back was being flogged. The smell of incense invaded his nostrils and seared the backs of his eyes. Unaccountably he recalled ice-cream and a loose filling dropping out. He looked uncertainly at two platters of wafers at the back of the aisle, sidled between them and edged into a rear pew.

Father Jacko stood robed with his arms raised and his back to the congregation mumbling something. Beside him an altar boy surveyed the congregation without interest. Barry did the same. Two pink old English ladies, grey and decayed, knelt in the front pew. Behind them, a rather splendid military type man, probably an expatriate, stood at attention with his magnificent wife looming beside him. Scattered elsewhere were one or two others and just in front of Barry, a young holiday couple stood whilst their two children sat disconsolately fiddling with their fingers. Then Jacko turned around beaming, his eyes hugely magnified in his glasses and roared, "Christ is Risen!" There was a rather lukewarm response and Jacko surveyed his small band of English faithful. His rough peasant features looked even grubbier against his liturgical vestments. He announced in his thick accent that he was not going to preach a sermon but proceeded to do so. He passed some incomprehensible remarks about a vision of the Cross, about crosses which bore carts and sailed ships. Then he went on to inform the bewildered congregation that Christ would wash the feet of even those with four toes. Barry stirred uneasily, scraping fragments of dried cement from his nails.

The service continued and Barry, following in an English Missal, found much of it uncannily familiar until it came to the sacrament. The congregation filed out and queued in the aisle. Barry watched them open their mouths and saw the priest take a wafer from the platter which the altar boy had collected from the back of the church, and lay it on their tongues. It seemed easy enough, so out into the aisle stepped Barry, last in line and taking one careful step forward each time a communicant was dispatched. At his turn Barry stepped forward and opened his mouth as if he were a performing seal. Father Jacko mumbled some words and then peered down hazily into the platter.

There was an awkward silence whilst Barry stood expectant with his mouth opened and beginning to dribble slightly. The priest hissed through his teeth and tutted. He looked urgently over his shoulder to the altar and back to Barry.

"We haven't enough ... Did you? At the back of the church?" he whispered.

Barry's mouth closed sharply. He clearly didn't understand the problem.

"It's all right. There's another plate load at the back of the church. I'll go and get it." And he turned around to fetch the wafers from the rear of the nave.

"No! They're not consecrated," Jacko whispered loudly enough for everyone to hear. This was the signal for the entire congregation to offer advice. One of the old ladies thought there might be some on the altar and Jacko bustled about at her direction. The looming lady in the second pew believed there might be some behind the curtain.

"There shouldn't be," Jacko groaned as he dithered irresolutely until he was eventually bullied into disappearing behind the curtain. Barry stood mildly spectating the strange rites as the curtain flapped and was rummaged in. Once Father Jacko's frightened face suddenly peered out like some stage act awaiting his cue and retreated before the orders of the woman in the second row. Clearly there was no more consecrated bread to be had.

"Can't you do some more?" Barry suggested, trying to be helpful. Jacko defeated, sorrowfully shook his head.

"Just have a little wine instead. You're probably a Protestant anyway," Jacko whispered, eyeing the second row nervously. There was a significant and disapproving 'Humph' from the second pew, but Barry said he didn't mind and he drank deeply from the chalice that Jacko held to his lips.

"You should have taken a wafer for yourself and put it in the platter as you came in," the looming lady snapped as she surged out past Barry, who was pretending to be praying in order to keep his head down.

Father Jacko, still disconcerted, continued glancing anxiously about him and was wishing everyone a Happy Christmas at the door until he was corrected by one of the disconsolate children, who seemed to have brightened up considerably. Barry stepped out blinking into the sunlight and the priest took his hand in his rough paws and clasped it warmly.

"I'm so glad you came," he said. "There's another Englishman here who helped me with some repairs this morning. I was hoping he would come too. Come and see."

And he ushered Barry to the statue of Christ washing St Peter's feet.

"Ah," he sighed. "Still only four toes. I thought Jesus might perform a miracle and make another one. But if he doesn't mind, why should we?"

The Thirteenth Stage

"St Paul brought Christianity to this island two thousand years ago but still they are not Christians." The angry young Gozitan glared at Barry as if challenging him to disagree, but Barry had nothing to say.

Outside on the ferry's deck the afternoon sun shone. Having explored Gozo fairly thoroughly over the last couple of years, he had gone over to Malta on a day trip and had been effectively abducted by two merry widows on the same outing. They had laid siege to him whenever they had encountered him in Gozo. He had frozen when he had seen them on the ferry this morning and had hidden in a shelter on the deck with a can of oil and some rusted chains. They had found him however, and hauled him out, reprimanded him for getting lost and promised him not to let him slip away again.

One of these widows was now tapping excitedly on the grimy glass, trying to attract his attention.

Barry didn't dare move his head. On one hand he was afraid to offend the angry Gozitan and on the other he was afraid of the gaping cleavage and the bust wrapped round by a mainsail of a blouse and knotted up high above the navel. The two jolly middle-aged widows had sat on either side of him on the coach trip around Malta, instructing him that they were all going to have a lot of laughs together. From then on, they had never ceased to nudge him, prod him, tease him and remind him of what a fun time they were all having. Amid their laughter and carping, his jaw had gulped around vainly for something witty to say in the spirit of their banter. All he had ever managed was the odd monosyllable or an "I dunno" and they had cackled hysterically and prodded him harder. Whether the Gozitan required some clever reply he was not sure.

He risked a movement of the eye towards the window and was greeted with a grin as large and fleshy as the cleavage.

"Porpoises," she was mouthing, "come and see the porpoises." Barry grinned weakly but he was trapped in the damp salty shadows of the snack bar by the Gozitan's morose tale.

"They go to church and say the Peace to one another and then they say bad things behind their backs; and the priests, they give us the Peace in church and Hell outside," the speaker continued, darkly contemplating the vinegary white wine at the bottom of his plastic cup.

Again, the eager knuckles and the swinging bosoms at the window were motioning him out, but Barry shrugged back helplessly. The young Gozitan's brown eyes scowled angrily out from beneath his tumbling black curls.

"See," he slapped the front page of the newspaper.

"The Pope visits here next month. He will drive past my shop to the Shrine of our Lady of Sorrows. It has been a dusty track for a hundred years. Now they lay tarmac so he won't get the bumps and they won't let us use it in case we spoil the tar. The priest calls and says I must paint my shop. I say my daughter is sick, she never gets well. She is back in hospital again. My shop loses money, I cannot afford it. He says I should sell T-shirts of the Holy Father and cardboard periscopes so that the faithful will all get a good view. Two thousand years of Christianity and we need cardboard periscopes to see the Pope!"

He gulped down the dregs of his wine and stood up. His open shirt stretched tightly across his stomach which lolled out over the belt of his jeans. A gold crucifix gleamed against his leathery chest. The ferry lurched slightly and there was a roar of engines and a flurry of water as it back-paddled.

"We are docking now," he announced, standing up and stretching stiffly. Despite his paunch he had narrow hips but none of the swagger the other young men seemed to have. Instead he moved heavily and sullenly towards the door with his burden of a sick child, failing business and loss of religious faith. All of these grievances he had unloaded onto Barry just because Barry had been sitting beside him. He had obviously forgotten that he had offered a lift to the three English travellers. The merry widows had started the conversation with the handsome dark-eyed man but had left it as soon as it had become sombre. However, they converged on him now. Barry could see them through the filthy windows of the ferry's cafeteria, surrounding him and loading him with their bags of shopping.

The chains rattled and the drawbridge clanked down. Barry hung back, sneaking behind a girder as the women scanned the deck for him. He prayed that Gozo was a big enough island for him to avoid them in the future. He saw them shrug and squeeze into a tiny Fiat parked beside the jetty. When at last the rusted old car had bounced on its tired springs across the dock and growled with its fleshy freight up the hill, Barry disembarked, watched the last puff of grey smoke from the exhaust pipe and boarded a minibus with the name of his hotel on the side.

After depositing the two guffawing English women in the square in Victoria, and receiving a farewell poke in the ribs, Marc lurched along the rutted dusty track the Pope would not be taking.

Nevertheless, the papal yellow and white was everywhere and his Holiness eyed him benignly from walls and balconies. The car now rode higher on its springs and lurched from one side of the road to the other. Marc's head felt bloated with the wine and he concentrated hard on his driving, trying to align his front wing with the long stretch of broken wall that edged the road. Checking that no police were about, he joined the new road and noted with some satisfaction that the tarmac was already crumbling at the edges. More worrying were the dusty tyre marks he left which would lead tellingly to his door. He decided he didn't care, especially when he noted another set of tracks leading along the pristine road surface to the old black Mercedes of Father Thomas parked outside his shop.

At the far end of the shop the priest and Josephine were talking conspiratorially. They looked up guiltily as Marc's silhouette loomed across the harsh sunlight of the doorway. He heard the till drawer being pushed closed with a suppressed click and, as his eyes became accustomed to the dimness of the interior, he noticed that both the priest and the altar boy with him were in their surpluses and that the boy had the incense with him.

"The Father has come to bless our shop and our home," Josephine's voice was thin and shaky. "He says it will help Margaret get better ... and the business ... and ..."

53

"Your temper and hardness of heart," Father Thomas added, a sarcastic smile creasing the smooth round face.

"Put that money you have stolen back in the till!" Marc roared, causing the altar boy to look up in alarm from the liquorice he was contemplating.

"Josephine, haven't I said that every cent he steals is medicine we cannot buy!"

He flung aside the beaded curtains behind the counter and disappeared into the living quarters beyond. He heard the priest muttering to Josephine the inevitable warning that the good parishioners would not patronise a shop run by a man outside the bosom of the Church, before hustling his altar boy outside and away from the contaminated liquorice.

Josephine entered the cool narrow room where they lived. She avoided her husband's fierce eyes.

"Have you been to the hospital?" he asked, softening a little.

"They say she must have more tests. How did you get on in Malta?"

"My brother can spare a little money. Not much. Not enough."

He watched his wife filling a pan. Her skin was rough like the earth outside and she was broadening at the hips. Under her eyes were dark hollows caused by months of peering into a desolate future. He thought of the two English women with their layers of pink speckled flesh and their hoarse laughter. Then he thought of the priest with his pink hand reaching out for money from the till and looked at his own – hard, stony like the limestone cliffs above.

"I am going onto the ridge to shoot," he announced. "Charlie says he heard turtle doves up there this morning."

He took the shotgun from the wall and rummaged in a drawer for cartridges.

"Yes, you listen to bad men like that Charlie, who make you godless, and you won't listen to the priest," Josephine suddenly cried out before her voice trailed off into angry sobs. Marc resolutely stuffed cartridges into each little pocket of his bandolier, ignoring her as she whimpered behind him.

"The Father says Margaret will not get better, and business will not get better until you come to Mass and pray to our Lady."

Marc crashed his gun down onto the table and twisted round on her.

"Business is bad because he orders the people not to come into the shop. So, they walk on past another half mile to Mrs Grech's who was about to retire and sell up. But the priests tell her to carry on and make big profits from my customers. But now I stock American magazines. The men will come in for the American magazines," he roared triumphantly.

"Huh!" Josephine stamped her foot. "Well, Father Thomas has taken your American magazines. I would not soil my hands with them."

Marc's face contorted with fury. His breath came thick and rasping in his throat. Grabbing his gun, he pushed past his wife out into the shop where the top magazine shelf was bare. Then with a shout of anger he flung himself outside. The priest's car was gone and the evening air was still. Far along the shining tarmac road he heard the Mercedes changing gear on the bend. Then it was quiet and only the sound of his breathing, heavy, eventually slowing, could be heard. An old woman plodded wearily up the hill, an empty shopping basket clutched against her faded black dress. Seeing him there darkly blocking the doorway she hesitated, then turned her head and trudged on past. The priest was right. There would be very little business: no permission to sell T-shirts or periscopes, no American magazines. Mrs Grech would have the monopoly of all the Papal souvenirs and make a good profit, minus of course a percentage to the church. He remembered himself telling someone on the ferry, "The priests give you the Peace in the church, then Hell outside it." If he ever said that here his wife would cry and rage at him. It had been good to vent it to someone silent and taciturn, who didn't seem to appreciate the scale of the blasphemy, or who didn't care.

With his bandolier round his waist and his uncocked gun under his arm he began the long climb up towards the ridge. Occasionally he stopped for breath and looked back to the flaking paint of his shop and the faded clothes drying on the roof. Now the sight irritated him and he was glad to reach the summit, from where his home was just a caustic white block on the tarmacked ribbon of road. The sun was slipping like a silver plate into the sea and a light evening breeze brushed the fennel against his legs releasing a slight aniseed smell. To his left bird nets were out. A square of terrace was marked out with rough stone pillars. On the top of each was a flat stone and perched on that a small cage with little twittering linnets hopping about. He skirted well clear of them and came round to a crude stone igloo beyond the traps. Inside was the glow of a cigarette which he knew would be Charlie, the "bad man" as Josephine called him. Charlie cursed the priests and lived in a boat house with a peeling boat and another man's wife.

"Your daughter is bad again?" Charlie asked as Marc squeezed in and squatted beside him. "I saw the big black car outside your shop. 'Marc won't like that,' I said to myself."

"Sure. The priests give us the Peace in the church and Hell outside," Marc said, now proud of his epigram. Charlie liked it. He chortled and was still repeating it to himself when Marc crawled out of the shelter and walked along the rim of the cliff, his gun raised against his shoulder looking for turtle doves.

At his feet the jagged limestone fell away in great pock-marked vertebrae and scars. Lower down, beans and potatoes clung to narrow terraces. To his right a stark, white stone cross seemed to erupt against the purple evening cloud. At its feet the body of Jesus was being cradled by Mary and a disciple. Marc had wandered over towards the Stations of the Cross which wound up the hill from the Shrine of Our Lady of Sorrows. The Pope would not be coming up as far as this. The limit of his pilgrimage was to be the Thirteenth Station – Jesus collapsing while carrying the cross. Beyond this the pathway was considered too rugged, so at the feet of the fallen Christ the Pope would conduct a short blessing and the shrine would be dedicated. The workmen had been busy carving out elegantly dressed stone steps, inserting a handrail, planting shrubs and washing down the statues. They were not going to bother smoothing the way beyond the Fallen Christ, however, so the last few stations remained rough and overgrown, and in the weeds lay the workmen's debris: burst cement bags, split buckets, a broken shovel.

Marc paused at the summit and looked down to where the path wound helter-skelter round the hillside through the broken rocks and thistles; and then the smooth white manicured part where the Pope would walk, down past the various stations to the great church below. He clambered down a few yards into some rough scree beneath Christ being lifted down from the cross to wait for the turtle doves which sometimes roosted here among the scrub in the evenings, undisturbed by the prospect of any papal visit.

An ancient carob tree grew just across the path and Marc pushed aside the long dangling pods and sat in underneath it. The ancient grey trunk was twisted into knotted arches supporting a heavy canopy above him. He didn't need the shade. The sun had now dipped into the horizon, stinging the sea with a welt of light and leaving the hillside a cool spreading purple. He liked this spot. He could sit here and be angry without having to justify it to anyone, while Mary and the disciple unloaded the cross just over the track above him. And if the turtle doves flew in from grazing in the fields below, well, he could shoot them.

As the shadows deepened he became more aware of the pale, sculptured face of the dead Jesus cushioned on his mother's lap. The rigor mortis of his empty eyes seemed fixed on the hunter skulking in the green gloom beneath the carob tree. Because it had not been considered necessary to clean up this statue it was marked by more than the passion of His crucifixion. There was the passion of cold nights and remorseless heat, of accumulated dirt and the blown sand that stung in the wind and of the rain that dripped from the thorns in the crown. There were streaks of grime and algae where tears should be and flaking plaster and grazed knees.

Marc glared back at Jesus, half in sorrow and half in accusation for his daughter lying ill again in hospital and he saw the wordless grief carved in the faces of the disciples. At the base of the statue was a small shrine of a few abandoned wild flowers and a jam-jar in which a candle glimmered, as remote and isolated as Charlie's cigarette in the crude stone hide. Marc tensed, resisting the usual sign of devotion, but not having to maintain his defiance in front of anyone, he gave in and crossed himself reluctantly. "In church they give us the Peace and outside they -" he was muttering bitterly to himself when suddenly, where the path performed a downward hairpin and looped round beneath him, there was a spurt of pink and grey and a flapping of wings. Instinctively Marc lifted his gun and fired. The loud retort echoed round the cliffs, coming back to him at the same time as he heard his shot rattling against some hard surface lower down the path.

It was a sound Marc couldn't recognise. He scrambled out from his hiding place and trotted off down the path, an uncertain frown on his dark brows. The rough path descended past the tableau of the crucifixion, past where the soldiers were nailing Christ's hands to the cross to where everything had been cleared and smartened up. Here, where the Pope was due to halt and hold his mass, where Christ was staggering beneath the weight of His cross, Marc halted too.

The path had wound right round the hill in a descending circle to within a short distance below the carob tree. Marc noted how the track had been rolled and the loose stones cemented into a neat wall. A soft honey coloured light illumined the stone figures, mellowing the agony of the Christ slumped beneath his great load. Marc's increasing sense of foreboding seeped out as sweat on his forehead. He had shot Jesus. The pellets from Marc's gun had sprayed the fallen Christ. Little black dents and chippings peppered his shoulders and chest. Now he had been shot, the single arm which supported Jesus should fold and the figure should collapse fatally. Nails and spear would not be needed. But no blood ran from the bullet holes and the Saviour bore the extra pain with no change in expression. His sharp stone features remained still, intent upon their unalterable crawl to Golgotha up above from where Marc had fired.

The gunman looked round in alarm. All was empty. The crags remained impassive, the pods from the carob tree still hung indifferently. The Pope would stop and see the shot marks. He would enquire how they had got there and no one would be able to explain how Jesus, despite his washing and scrubbing, now carried the scars of Marc's anger on his trek to the cross. And he hadn't even flinched. The great blasphemy made Marc shudder. It was one thing arguing with Father Thomas, but shooting Jesus was another. He sank to his knees among the filigree leaves of fennel and crossed himself, urgently fingering the gold cross at his throat.

Then, with the gun over his shoulder he set off in a panic down the path, past the flogging and the trial and the arrest. It was as if something had been expiated and that the fallen Jesus could bear a little more pain. Marc realised that his anger and fear had dispersed, so he slowed down, his steps became lighter and jauntier, and his narrow hips swaggered as they had not done for many weeks now.

At the foot of the path he met Father Jacko, the one priest with whom he could have friendly words. He could see the weak eyes dilating and peering through the thick glasses until Marc was close enough to recognise. The sun-beaten face broke into a smile.

"Ah, it's you, Marc. I heard your shot. Did you hit anything?" he asked in a friendly, matter-of-fact sort of way. The irony of the question amused the young huntsman.

"Yes, I did," he laughed and clapped the priest on the back. "I hit Jesus and he didn't mind, but Father Thomas will and he'll give me Hell if he finds out." He quickly related the events of the day, climaxing his tale with his angry shot at the turtle dove. Jacko looked grave.

"And Father Thomas will give me Hell too," he sighed ruefully. "It's my job to walk up here every day and make sure everything is tidy, undamaged and free from litter and now you tell me you have shot Jesus to pieces where His Holiness will stop and hold mass!" Then Jacko chuckled because he saw that a crude piece of peasant carving and a pop-shot at a turtle dove had saved a man.

"Never mind," he said. "I know a man, an Englishman who repairs things. A little filler, a little sandpaper. His Holiness will never know. In fact, I think he would be pleased if he did."

Doing Business

This was the third consecutive Easter Week in which Francis the estate agent had to write off entire days as wasted. He even put a cross through the week on his calendar, and wrote 'Wasted' in angry red biro. It was inevitable that Barry would call and ask to be driven round any likely looking properties on the island. "Just a small place," he echoed every year, "plenty of sun. View. Nice walk down to the sea."

Each year Francis had shown him such places: new flats with balconies and Corinthian columns facing over the harbour, compact apartments, narrow and shaded in new developments, old farmhouses jostling over the edges of gorges with prickly pear and tamarisk trees, dusty new shells of houses in un-weathered yellow rearing up from stacks of cut stone. At each one Barry would get out of the estate agent's BMW, kick around a little, sniff, tap walls and grunt, "I dunno, p'haps I ought to wait a year or so."

From the annual bumpy rides around Gozo, Francis knew the state of his client's finances. Barry had worked for forty years without having to spend a penny on rent or mortgage. He had no hobbies, no vices and no luxuries except for his annual expedition to buy a place in the sun. He did general handiwork and worked overtime to avoid going home to his mother and someone called Albert. His savings had mounted remorselessly, interest piling upon capital and he would be a cash customer. Sometimes when they had stopped at a particularly appealing prospect, a restored house looking down a terraced valley or a renovated fisherman's cottage in a hidden bay maybe, Francis had probed Barry's prospects by mentioning large sums of money. Once, as an experiment, Francis had indicated a villa with a swimming pool and suggested a sum commensurate with a celebrity or Mafia boss and Barry hadn't even flinched.

Instead Barry would furtively open his building society passbook and contemplate the figures which streamed down the pages and mutter, "I dunno, I dunno, there must be summat. But you never know. Summat might happen. Maybe I should work another year or two, no point in rushing," and he would shake his head mournfully at the possible apocalypse which might suddenly denude his passbook of its columns and zeros.

Francis was also planning to retire. Just another year or two. Just another fat commission or so.

Perhaps he and Barry were not so different. This realisation made him less patient with his client. And he had another one as well – Mrs Grech. For four years now, her general store had been on his books and every time he brought a prospective customer she had waivered and decided not to sell just yet. Either profits were looking up or she was feeling better than she had done in years. Just another year. Wait until things fall off again.

Barry had asked to be dropped off by the Stations of the Cross. Francis couldn't think why. He wouldn't be allowed to walk up the immaculate steps where the Pope was due to walk in a few weeks. As the BMW jolted across the hills on the dusty, unmade road, they could already see the yellow and white bunting decking houses below; except that the strong sun was relentlessly bleaching the yellow so that by the time His Holiness should arrive there would only be white pennants to greet him.

At the foot of the hill Barry disembarked, mumbled something about maybe next year, no point in rushing and strolled towards the ascent. At the first station Francis could see his brother, Jacko, sitting in the fennel, a spear of grass in his mouth, his eyes closed to the sun and his legs spread under the tattered soutane. Francis eased the car away so as not to be seen by him. Jacko, like Barry and Mrs Grech, was part of the conspiracy to humiliate him and prevent him from ever becoming a leading business man. Leading business men rose above the wiles and idiosyncrasies of peasants. But he couldn't. He had to be content with the outward shows of success: a BMW, a tie, a suit and a clean shirt, albeit with sweat marks under the armpits. He was insolubly linked to a dissolute priest who lounged all day in the clover or sat in seedy bars playing cards with the locals.

His fellow professional classes, the lawyers and bankers, couldn't take him entirely seriously whilst his brother made a public spectacle of himself. There had been talk of his climbing over balconies, assaulting naked Maltese girls and many business lunches had been enlivened by jokes about sopranos and sandals. Yet Francis wished to present himself as a success and felt he didn't deserve to have the business community associating him with Jacko like that. On the other hand, because of his brother, the peasants trusted Francis's integrity and good sense, as if it were a family trait. Francis knew he didn't deserve their trust and faith either. On a small island he couldn't disavow the connection, so he had spent a career trying to reform his wayward brother and occasionally importing his sister from the mainland to assist.

Without disturbing Jacko, he drove the half-mile up the hill intending to go back to his office in Victoria past Mrs Grech's general store. He drew up wearily outside the shop. It was as he had half expected – his estate agent's sign was missing. The sun sprawled in a soft apricot warmth across the sand coloured front of the building. Geraniums and bougainvillea mingled and trickled down in pert reds and purples from the balcony of her living quarters above the store. Francis took a deep breath. This was to be the final confrontation. He was going to remove her from his books once and for all.

All across the island there was a building boom, a race to beat the planning restrictions that would inevitably come. Open shells of unfinished buildings gaped down on all the harbours and little beaches. Beauty spots had been excavated and concrete foundations put down and abandoned. Francis glanced down the blue valley which tumbled steeply to the sea. It was too steep for development and there were too many stubborn peasants who farmed it for a pittance of rent that they paid to the church. There was so much for an estate agent to think about, so many problems and risks, yet the promise of such rewards if only the Europeans would come flooding in! It was worth giving it another year or so. Yet he couldn't be distracted by the unpredictability and thwarting of local peasants like Mrs Grech, when there were major German developers and Anglo-Maltese consortia to be negotiated with.

He found his For Sale sign dumped behind a broken stone wall among some thistles and donkey dung. He tore it free vehemently, pricking himself and soiling his white shirt-cuffs, and flung it into the boot of his car. Mrs Grech came tap-tapping with her stick out of the olive-violet shadows of her shop and watched him. Her face was as grey and cracked as the wall Francis had clambered over. Great pins stuck out of her hair bun and her widow's black, shiny with wear, had sheen in the sunlight like the coat of a black beetle.

"What are you doing?" she snapped, her voice harsh and sepulchral in her throat.

"I've had enough," shouted Francis as the sweat stung his eyes. "I keep putting this notice up because you want to sell and you keep taking it down because you don't want to sell. When you decide to retire or die, sell it yourself!"

"Well, this is not a good time," she reasoned, settling herself heavily onto a crude bench beside the door. "The young couple down the hill are in trouble with the priests and all their customers come here now. Beside I have the only concession here to sell all the papal souvenirs. Maybe when the Holy Father has been, or when the summer is over ... or when -"

"I don't care when," interrupted Francis getting into his car, slamming the door and gesticulating through the open window. "There are other estate agents. Go and bother them. It's not good for anybody's business for people to see their signs dumped on a pile of donkey dung!" With a final scowl and a wave of the fists he roared off whilst Mrs Grech shrugged and closed her eyes as the sweet scent of aniseed and cut clover wafted up the valley.

Meanwhile, having been forced off the usual road by ecclesiastical injunctions, Francis found himself cutting across the hill on a stony and hard-rutted track. He gritted his teeth as he felt the axle of his BMW scraping the ground but he eventually came to the abandoned farmhouse he had seen from below. He asked some locals who the owners were. It was not a good prospect, barely distinguishable from the decayed walls and rubble around it. The owners would probably use the stone to build themselves a new place – one day – when they got around to it.

Anyway, the enquiries wasted another hour and so he was particularly frustrated when the rough hillside track descended to the main road from the Shrine and came to a halt with a chain across the road, some old oil-drums and a sign saying 'Road Closed'. Steaming to himself, Francis turned the car around rather awkwardly and retraced his irritating route. He would have to pass that harpy with the stick, Mrs Grech again, his brother idling somewhere and perhaps even the gormless Englishman.

In fact, he passed Barry at the door of Mrs Grech's shop. Barry had been shown some pellet scars on the statue of Christ carrying the cross and had agreed that a bit of sandpaper and some filler would do the job. He had asked for them in Marc's shop, but it seemed to have very little stock of anything. Besides, Marc, whom he vaguely remembered from the ferry, went into a diatribe about priests which he had heard before.

"Go to Mrs Grech," he had roared, "she has everything: sandpaper, filler, God's blessing, the favour of the Church, concessions for holy periscopes, my customers, American magazines under her counter ..."

Whilst Jacko nodded sympathetically and made a few restraining comments, Barry just gazed at the empty shelves and the sallow complexioned wife with the tired hollows around her eyes. He remembered something about a sick daughter. Besides, Marc had drifted into Maltese. The exaggerated shrugs and ferocious arm waving made language a little redundant but Barry waited patiently with no idea of what Marc was saying.

"If she retired and sold up all the people would come back here. They have nowhere else to go, despite what the priests say. And the priests would have to give me the concessions for the Pope's visit, they would have no choice. I could build up my stock on the profits, get good credit and pay the medical bills. But she won't retire whilst she's on to a good thing."

"Go to Mrs Grech," he suddenly yelled in English waving his arms wildly, and Barry startled from his reverie and not having understood a word, to Mrs Grech's he went.

For Francis, there was no escaping his brother at the bottom of the hill. He was standing in the middle of the road squinting into the sun as if looking for someone.

"Have you seen the Englishman?" Jacko enquired, bending stiffly to speak through the window when he had at last recognised who the driver was. "He went up to Mrs Grech's to buy – " but Jacko recollected himself and divulged no more. The shooting of Christ confessed to him by some reckless and angry young man had the status of the Sacrament for him.

The day was now totally wasted anyway, so Francis was persuaded to join Marc, Jacko and one or two other loungers sitting around the odd plastic tables Marc had set out in the shade of the mulberry trees. Having decided to abandon any hope of a productive day, he allowed himself to be drawn into their carefree idleness, the desultory chatter, the deep, sharp, red wine which someone uncorked. And the sun, as hot as iron in the Easter sky, glared down on the mulberry trees beneath which the men sat, while Father Jacko took out a pack of cards from under his dusty soutane and poured a glass from the wine that Marc had just opened and passed it to his brother. After a while the sun slowly turned milky and a gentle breeze rustled up from the sea, fingers of light fluttering down through the mulberry leaves. Francis took off his tie and was half dozing, dreaming of a retirement beneath the shade of mulberry trees, when Barry returned, sat down with them and announced in his few sparing words, "I've just bought that ole shop up the road. Plenty of sun. View. Nice walk down to the sea. Negotiated with her direct and went over her price if she'd close down straight away. No time like the present."

Then he noticed Francis, sitting erect, ashen, his mouth lolling open. "Sorry about the trouble," Barry explained to him, "but she said she ain't got no estate agent. 'Strike while the iron's hot', I always say."

Touching Up
St Catherine

Father Jacko tried to appear as if he were examining the plaster statue of St George at the street corner. The votive candle from the night before was quietly spluttering on its dying wick as the morning sun trickled like melted butter down the high stone walls. St George wore a bland smile on his doll-like face as he impaled the rather harmless looking dragon at his feet.

"You seem strangely interested in St George this morning, considering you pass by him at least twice a day!"

If a voice could have a shadow then this was it.

"Ah, yes. It's very … uhmmm …" but Jacko knew he was caught out. From the cool shade of the corner he squinted along the narrow street to where Sister Terror loomed monstrous against the glare of the morning sun. To step out of the shade towards her was to step into a grilling of heat and scolding words. The street was a deep gulley of golden stone, its cobbles baked for a few hours by the sun as it squeezed between the church tower and a high balcony. Then, as it moved round a cool purple shadow would again creep along the street's length. But for now, it was blocked by the terrifying Sister Theresa, arms akimbo and an acid smile on her wimpled face.

"The ladies have already gone to their prayers, you'll be pleased to know, Father."

"Err ... Which ladies are these?" Jacko stammered rather unconvincingly.

"Why – the ladies you and half your colleagues come sniffing round every time you hear the chapel bell, hoping to gawk or get a whiff of perfume as they pass across the street to Mass," the sister sneered.

Poor Father Jacko splayed his hands and swallowed and gulped his innocence of what she meant, but she clearly hadn't finished. She bent her head towards him so he had to blink away the spray of her invective.

"And thank you for your kind letter offering to be their new chaplain. I filed it with at least two dozen others but the privilege has been given to dear Father Jerome, who, as you know, is 87 and blind and far more suited to be a minister to our Sisters of Abjuration than you and all your dribbling friends."

The Sisters of Abjuration. Oh, the Sisters of Abjuration! How often did Jacko and some of his less saintly colleagues speculate about the Sisters of Abjuration: wealthy widows, mistresses or divorcees who, having conjured with the fleshly desires of men, for mysterious reasons had now had renounced all male intercourse and sealed themselves away from masculine eyes. This was considered to be a particularly holy abjuration made all the more saintly by their renunciation of what they had once enjoyed, and more exotic by the secret knowledge that was locked away with them.

For a moment Jacko imagined a passing perfume and the whisper of a dress brushing the portal of the chapel. But the smell of Sister Theresa's breath and the stiff crinkle of her bulky habits eradicated all such delusions.

Recollecting himself, Jacko straightened himself and clasped his hands before him in what he calculated was a more pious but business-like manner.

"Yes, quite, quite," he mumbled. "But, now, Sister Terror, I mean Theresa, I thought I would just check that the arrangements for the children's visit today are ..."

The convent door was open. Through a cool marble hallway, he glimpsed a courtyard of infinite promise where sunlight flickered through the gently swaying shadows and a fountain played into a stone pool. He could almost inhale the fragrance of lemon and of the bougainvillea spilling over a balcony. For a moment, he was lulled by the sound of water and the humming of a woman's voice. But then Sister Theresa meaningfully pulled the door shut.

"All the arrangements have been made with their art teacher. You know they have," she snarled. "You are chaperone. Just make sure none of those teenage hussies come with their short skirts and naked shoulders. Carmel Bergini is a young man of exceptional piety and purity. He is destined for the priesthood. We do not want him being distracted."

She eyed him significantly until he turned and retreated back to St George's corner before she hammered on the great convent door with its brass handle and iron hinges. A tiny grill slid open, there was a lifting of latches and after one last check on the priest she was admitted.

Madam Vella, the art teacher, was a scampering, perpetually distracted little woman invariably dressed in smock top and long skirt spotted with dabs of paint and dried clay. She led her students into the narrow street and paused at the chapel door.

"Now," she chirruped, "we are enormously privileged to see Carmel Bergini at work. He has restored paintings in the Vatican itself. That means he cleans them and repaints the damaged parts himself.

Just imagine what skill that takes!" she paused for a rhetorical effect that was not forthcoming.

All heads were turned as a fast clattering of stiletto heels on the cobbles announced the late arrival of Pietra Azzopardi, her tight school blouse struggling to contain its contents and her tiny skirt little more than a gesture at uniform. Madam Vella eyed her with alarm and Jacko groaned audibly, his eyes fixed on the legs until he realised that their owner was grinning mischievously at him. Quickly he shook his head with exaggerated disapproval.

"Er ... some of you will need to take a shawl from the box in the porch to er ... umm," Madam Vella mumbled, scrutinising the long offending limbs. "Father Jacko will ensure proper ... er ... um ..." and a little shiver passed through her as she recalled herself to her introductory talk.

"It has been said of Carmel Bergini," she continued, referring now to some crumpled notes she had retrieved from her pocket, "that only an artist of unimpeachable piety and spiritual purity would be able to capture the original rapture of the artist and restore his holy vision to the canvas and that," here she once more paused for rhetorical effect but upon catching sight of the thighs again she lost her train of thought and shuffled though her notes. "It has been said of Carmel Bergini ... that ... that ... Carmel Bergini is such a man," she finished rather lamely.

Into the chapel's dark liquid gloom and pungent aroma of incense the class tramped. Father Jacko was ensuring that each student was decently attired and pursuing Pietra Azzopardi down the aisle, imploring her to take a shawl.

"To wrap ... er ... around ... but ... I think ... you should."

The girl looked at the offered garment with some disdain, then smiled cheekily at the priest and, with a toss of her long dark hair and hips a-swaying, carried the shawl over her arm to where some spotlights had been erected to illuminate the picture that was being restored.

Madam Vella was ducking and bowing and clasping her hands prayerfully before and behind her as she introduced Carmel Bergini who stood smiling beatifically. He was everything an aspiring saint should be. His curly black hair was tousled and flecked with paint and the sanctified hands he was carefully wiping on a cloth were delicate and pale. The girls watched his hand movements as if that cloth were to one day become a relic. Under the intensive spots his dark eyes sparkled with points of light and his face glowed with radiance. The girls crept in closer, nudging into the shadows, hanging on his every word.

The picture, he explained was a nineteenth century copy of the Execution of St Catherine, currently in a museum in Amsterdam. In soft tones he invited the students to examine the anachronistic costumes and the somewhat rigid expressions of the characters. He indicated the blessed smile of St Catherine as she knelt before her executioner and invited the students to describe the expression on the executioner's face, which, he prompted, was rather more human and earthly than the rest.

"I think he fancies her," Pietra volunteered, somehow having squirmed her way to the front of the group. The shawl that was meant to hide her legs was now tied rather coquettishly round her neck.

"It is a look of reverence and respect," Madam interjected loudly, "he is clearly reluctant to carry out his role."

Carmel Bergini drew his sleeve across his mouth and nodded rather ambiguously before going on to explain how he had to use certain solvents to remove the accumulated grime and candle smoke from the canvas and then had to mix his paint in the same way as the artist and use exactly the same directions of brush stroke. Finally, he announced that he needed to get back to his work, that some attention needed to be given to the broken spokes of the wheel that were scattered at the foot of the painting. He bowed to Madam, his curly hair flicking in the light and took her hand in his divine miracle-working fingers. She almost curtsied, flustered and blushing. They all watched in hushed reverence as he lay on his side at the foot of the picture frame and began with almost imperceptible movements of a scraper to work at the grease and dust that was lodged there.

Led by their teacher, the group slowly dispersed to look at some other artefacts in the chapel, but Pietra lingered on, giving Jacko an opportunity to move alongside her and appeal to her to adjust her shawl properly. But she was now leaning across the recumbent figure of the young man examining the executioner closely.

"Why has he got that lump in his tights?" she suddenly asked.

It was precisely then that Jacko heard the boom of Sister Terror calling to the school party that it was time to leave.

"Carmel Bergini needs to work in quietness and devotion," she announced. "The sanctity of his task requires utmost concentration so please leave quietly." The harsh rap of her shoes on the flagstones was coming swiftly towards them.

Jacko gulped very hard. Unaccountably he seemed to be holding the shawl now in his hand and lurched towards the girl with it, knocking her off balance as he did so. Miraculously she was able to avoid impaling the young saint's face on her stiletto heel by stepping over him with one long bare leg so that when Sister Terror loomed out of the surrounding darkness, Pietra was standing astride the young saint who was staring up into what might have been construed as heaven or possibly hell.

"We were just trying to see how he removed the grime!!" Jacko blurted out in panic.

Carmel Bergini, having extricated himself sat back on his heels and graced Sister Theresa with the most beatific of smiles.

"It is so rewarding, don't you think, Sister, when these young people *show* so much ... er ..." he explained, then swallowing hard he added hurriedly, "I mean show so much *interest* in sacred art. But how I have been gifted with the skills to accomplish some of these things must remain a mystery of my trade." His smile and the blessed inclination of the head were clearly meant to dismiss the sister and his audience. A little thawing took place in Theresa's manner, flattered as she was by his melting smile and effusive piety.

"Yes, of course, but I think you ... er ... I mean *they* have seen enough," she whispered through her teeth, her eyes narrowing as she glared at Jacko and the miscreant girl.

A warm velvet darkness filled the street. At the corner the votive candle flickered beneath St George and a street lamp cast shadows on the wall. Father Jacko, passing the solid door of the Convent of Abjuration lingered a moment. Too much thick, acid, red wine lay in his stomach and all his senses seemed remote and disconnected. Then behind the door he thought he heard something that evoked in the mists of his imagination the call of peacocks, a breath of perfume and the sighing of shadows, the soft tread of bare feet on marble paving, the rustle of skirts and the phantasmagoria of a high combed mantilla passing like a galleon in the night. However there, from just behind the door there was definitely a giggling and whispering that was no dream. There really was. The mists and the fantasies dissolved. Alarmed, Jacko pressed his back into the shadows of the chapel wall as the door creaked open and a woman's voice escaped into the night. Carmel Bergini emerged looking back and laughing as the door was closed behind him. He turned and saw Jacko, held up a plastic bag of Brillo scouring pads and grinned.

"The mystery of my trade," he teased, one dark sparkling eye winking roguishly and off along the street he sauntered, raising the bag once again in salute as he disappeared round the corner under the meagre glow of the votive lamp.

The Priest's Love Song

The American magazine had been washed down the valley on the sluggish stream that was the last of the winter rains. The sun had bleached any sensuousness out of the centre-fold pin-up and she now straddled the baked rocks indifferently. An occasional flurry of water oozed through the staple holes and caused the page to belly upwards as if she were in the throes of some weary erotic gasp.

Father Jacko was edging his way sideways down the gully. He had the bandy-legged gait of a local peasant and the broad brown feet that clambered down the loose stones were indistinguishable from their worn leather sandals. He leaned heavily on the pillar of the bridge that supported the road across the stream and tried to lift the magazine with a long bamboo pole.

"The last of Father Thomas's winter harvest," he quipped to himself as he slowly and stiffly stretched out the long swaying pole trying unsuccessfully to extricate the offending literature from among the cans, plastic bottles and branches that had accumulated there.

The late April sun was turning from gently chiding warmth to bullying summer. As he leaned out wearily and tried to steady himself he felt the heat prickling through the thick woollen sweater his sister had knitted for him. "Wear it until May," he heard her scolding him, "or you'll be catching cold and sniffing and wiping your nose on your sleeve like you always do." The sky, pale blue, shimmered and flashed like aluminium as a car ground the gravel of the bridge above, a fierce spark of sunlight erupting in its windscreen.

Father Jacko lowered his bamboo pole and rested his old shoulders for a moment. Apart from the white band of collar at his weathered throat he could be any one of the peasant farmers hoeing their beans on the terraces above the valley. His face, the same dusty and furrowed brown of the fields around him, seemed to fold inward as he concentrated his poor eyesight on the idly flapping blur that was his target.

"Can we help you, Father?"

Two small boys, as brown and dusty as he, scuttled down from the road above, their bare feet impervious to the sliding stones and thistles. Father Jacko wiped his brow with his greasy navy beret and smiled while his hand felt for his usual rock among the clover. Here he sat amid the red nodding flowers and darting bees and squinted through his bottle bottom glasses at the boys paddling out into the stream.

"What is it, boys?" he asked, with little interest.

"It's nothing bad, Father," one called whilst they feverishly leafed through the pages, sniggering and whistling at the flanks of flesh sprawled across the damp paper.

The old man nodded knowingly. He allowed them a moment and then ordered them to spread the magazine out on a rock to dry. They seemed to know the routine well and did as they were told with a few quick furtive glances before sliding down through the clover and sitting on either side of the priest.

"What are you doing here?" the old man enquired, his voice rough and distant like a far-off saw. His gaze never shifted from the point below where the Mediterranean scooped inward into the small harbour.

"We came to ask you for help with our maths homework," one piped back. Deep behind the spectacles the feeble old eyes chuckled.

"It's the Easter holidays, you young liar. There are no more magazines here for you to gawk at," he muttered and the trio subsided into a convivial silence.

After a few minutes Jacko seemed to remember something and placing a huge leathern hand on the tousled black head of one of the boys, pulled it back and inspected the face slowly.

"Michael Grima," the boy said.

"And Johnny?" guessed the priest.

"Yes, Johnny," Michael replied.

Again, there followed a companionable silence as the priest's eyes probed the green and yellow-flecked valley to the harbour and followed the bundle of flat-roofed, sand-coloured houses that were stacked like shoe-boxes up the hill by the harbour's edge. Though his view was watery and dim he knew where the Grima house was, still just two storeys with its leaning balcony and flaking paint-work. Around it the traditional homes were sprouting extra storeys and a tangle of masts, aerials and satellite dishes.

"Your father no longer takes his boat out, I hear?"

"No, Father, he hires out cars and wind-surfers to the tourists."

"The cars he has no licenses for and the windsurfers he cannot ride. But he was a fine fisherman," the priest reflected.

"Tell me, how much per kilo do the restaurants pay for lampuki?" The boys looked blankly at him.

"Your father could tell me instantly and calculate his profit margins just like that." Father Jacko snapped his fingers peevishly.

"But if your father rents a car for 10 lira a day and a tourist wants to pay in pounds sterling and the exchange rate is 1.9 pounds to the lira, how much will he make in a week? That is the maths you will learn now."

Father Jacko's instinct for maths had drawn generations of school children to him when they needed help with their homework. He never concerned himself with the abstractions of the subject but simply worked out the answers for them. They understood, as he did, that the girls would marry young and make lace and babies, and the boys would bounce out to sea in their bright blue fishing boats with the intent yellow eyes on either side of the prow. The only maths they would need would be enough to calculate the profit on a swordfish or recognise a bargain in the market. Some, however, would find success on the mainland or emigrate to Canada, returning thirty years later with money in their pockets to buy and restore a farmhouse and look after their parents. Moreover they would be able to afford accountants. So, a succession of boys with varied futures before them, sought him and the American magazines out by the stream under the bridge, brought him their sums and paid with pickled onions, his only known vice. Here he would suck them and quietly belch, his distant eyes madly dilated by the massive lenses of his spectacles.

"Do you have matches?" Father Jacko enquired.

"Matches, Father?"

"Yes," he snapped back with mock impatience. "The matches you light your cigarettes with when you read the magazines under the bridge."

Michael blushed. "Father, what does Father Thomas do with the dirty magazines in the summer when the stream is dried up?" Johnny hid his face giggling, but the old man grinned.

"Like the Vision of Ta Pinu or the Holy Trinity, that's a mystery," he said and the boys reverted to silence while the clover swayed about them. Then Father Jacko described how Father Thomas conducted his seasonal raids on the newsagents and choirboys and cast the smutty plunder with great ritualistic loathing into the stream. From there the magazines lazily washed downhill, browsed by many a field labourer at his irrigation until, if Father Jacko didn't intervene, they would become snarled up rather publicly by the village bus stop where the stream ran through a grate under the road. As tiny black-headed warblers tumbled and chattered in the tamarisk trees and the magazines turned to ash, Father Jacko told the boys about love; of how they had mothers and sisters and the sweet Virgin Mary for their adoration; of how they would grow to love wives and children; of how the magazines were just sad, loveless things. He spoke of how men tried to buy the love of women with money but how Christ gave his love freely and paid for his bride the Church with his life. His song of love, of purity, of frailty and of more love mixed with the sound of doves and bees and the gentle evening breeze. He didn't muddle them with mysteries this time, but told them the answers as he did with their maths homework. Now there were no giggles as the boys gazed mistily down to the harbour, which seemed to be radiant with a holy fire as the sun sank below the rocky turret of the hill on which San Salvador stood, the shadows of his open arms stretching across the flat roofs of the houses. With his stick Jacko poked at the last pallid glimpse of buttock charring in the fire. "There it goes, poor thing," he whispered, sadly weary of human sin.

Back in the village, with the twilight deepening around the moored fishing boats, the boys erupted with excitement and raced across the nets that had been spread on the ground for repairing. An unusually expensive car was parked on the double yellow lines outside the hotel. It was guarded by a policeman who stood importantly beside it, a cigarette glowing in the cupped palm of his hand. Jacko looked with resignation over to the hotel and sighed. Beyond the automobile admirers he could see a small but eager crowd jostling in the dim lobby. Something was going on there, perhaps a wedding or some celebrity. At a table away from the group he could just make out two heads close together, conspiring. He was due to meet his brother and sister there. He had one hugely successful brother in London, attached to a bank; another hugely respected teaching in a seminary in Toronto; the brother whose outline he could now see was Francis, allegedly the principal estate agent in Gozo and the sister who, with huge acumen, had married a wealthy Maltese lawyer and not lifted an extravagantly ringed finger since.

Every so often she deemed it her filial responsibility to come to Gozo in order to remind Jacko what an embarrassment and disgrace he was to the family. There would be the usual litany of how grubby his soutane was, how dirty his feet were and how he smelled of pickled onions and garlic. The last visit had been in the wake of the scandal when he had tripped over a topless German woman on the beach. "You're supposed to be a priest," his sister had hissed, "like your fine Father Thomas clearing those whores from the beach, not rolling in the sand with them. And stop grinning!"

Another visit had been to pacify the fine Father Thomas after Jacko who, in his eagerness for a pickled onion after a rather long confirmation service, had leaned across the Bishop to grab a jar from the fridge. Unfortunately, the lid had not been screwed on properly and the Bishop had been liberally anointed with pickle.

"Father Thomas thinks you delayed his elevation to the Pro-Cathedral in Valletta by your gluttony and clumsiness. And stop grinning."

He felt it was important to be late so he wasted a few minutes joking with some old reprobates at the lottery kiosk as the evening darkened and the moon, sharp as a scimitar, cut the night sky behind San Salvador. Families in their best clothes promenaded up and down the harbour while a warm breeze from the sea gently billowed their white skirts and floated the aroma of salt, pizza and fish in the evening. Groups of young girls with long bare legs, the fairy lights sparkling in their black hair, paraded past and laughed at the lads astride their mopeds.

Jacko took a last look at where the moon sliced the warm night and prepared himself for the latest verbal bludgeoning.

"Joseph Spiteri at the hotel," the policeman informed him, his belly puffing out over his tight belt. "We've got to keep order. The women get excited."

As Jacko approached he could see his brother and sister, their heads bent closely together, obviously itemising his shortcomings. The candlelight flickering on the ornamental lobster pots above their heads added to the atmosphere of inquisition and inferno he anticipated.

His sister commenced her salvo with a well-practised prelude about his appearance. The beret was disgusting, the soutane stank and she was sure he had deliberately not changed into anything more respectable just to spite them. Whilst pleading innocence with his hands, Jacko smiled inwardly and wickedly. She was, of course, absolutely right.

"Do you know who's here?" she hissed at him confidentially, as he stood before them, head bowed, disgusting beret clutched before him like a naughty schoolboy, "Joseph Spiteri." The name articulated so decisively was meant to convey everything. Joseph Spiteri was a local boy who had made good in Malta and as far afield as Italy. He was a singer of sentimental songs devoted to his mother, the Holy Virgin and, more recently, to the young woman he had just married with much publicity. In the popular imagination, especially to his audience of mainly middle-aged women, he was identified with everything that was pure and romantic. It was even said that he might be singing in front of the Pope at Mass in the Basilica. Jacko was meant, of course, to note the contrast of Spiteri, successful, urbane and wholesome with himself, shameful, rustic and seedy.

"Why he wants to bring that beautiful girl back to a place like this on her honeymoon, I shall never know," she added, glancing up the stairs to the restaurant where the couple had disappeared.

They didn't offer him a drink but instead spirited him upstairs where there were fewer people in front of whom to feel degraded and where the pickled onion aroma was a little diluted by the evening air. The warm breeze creaked in the raffia awning and vines fluttered listlessly. Already the moon was perched high in the night and its reflection rippled across the waves towards them.

The terrace had a few tables set out and served as an extension to the restaurant. A lone figure sat, a napkin in his collar, dubiously clutching a knife and fork. He and the lobster on his plate exchanged mournful expressions. The estate agent brother pointedly kept his back to the diner.

"That Englishman," he growled. "A waster – like yourself, Jacko."

The celebrity and his new wife were also here, in a candle-lit alcove close and intent in their own newly married intimacies. A momentary expression of longing flickered across the sister's face as she glanced over and as inconspicuously as possible ushered her brothers along the inner wall to a table in the shadows.

The usual inventory of Jacko's deficiencies was recited and a stirring admonition delivered by the brother. The celebrity sat with his back to them with the girl facing him. Through the flexing candle shadows and his dim vision, Jacko could just see the heavy gold necklace that glimmered over her soft, honey-coloured breasts. Because he had to squint his eyes to see, his sister soon noticed.

"Stop gawping at that girl and listen to what your brother is saying," she snapped. "You're not fit to look at her anyway."

"I wonder if he's thinking of buying property here," ruminated the estate agent. "I hear he's into hotels and everything now. A commission on that and I could retire. I've worked hard. I'm sixty-four and I deserve it." He slapped his thighs with self-justification. The speech clearly implied that none of these statements applied to Jacko.

"I suppose you're still collecting dirty magazines," the sister was saying. Her closely curled coif was died dark henna and she patted it with her hand as she looked across at the massed blackness of the young bride's hair. "Did you see the wedding on TV?" she continued. "He looked so handsome in that white suit and she was so pure, a real virgin bride, like a princess." She sighed wistfully and surveyed the back of the celebrated singer as he whispered sweet things of love to his young wife. Then she recollected herself, pointedly informing Jacko of all the latest triumphs of other siblings, children, grandchildren and neighbours.

Now in the wickedness of his heart, in his pride and to his eternal shame, Jacko's revenge was stirred. He lifted his head for the first time.

"Hello, Joseph," he called.

Brother and sister froze in horror.

The singer turned.

"Ah, Father Jacko," he smiled, "I'm so glad you could come."

He rose, came over, and with the faintest scent of fine after-shave, bent slightly at the knee and kissed the knotted peasant fingers where the smell of onions still lingered.

"This man," he said to the sister without acknowledging her, "taught me everything that made my career. How to love and how to add up money," he chuckled.

And then to Father Jacko, "I'm glad you got my letter. You are why we are here. Please come and bless us."

So with great deference he led the little priest away from his gaping brother and sister to meet his bride. In the flickering candle light, they saw the chafed peasant lips lightly kiss the soft cheek that was offered, and through the rustling of the vines and the creaking raffia they heard the acclaimed TV star saying, "Here is the first man I ever heard sing about real love. Up there on the hillside by the stream where the magazines are laid out to dry."

Stardom

A swarm of 'chippies' had been sawing and hammering since early morning and by mid-afternoon the tiny chapel had been converted into a Greek temple. It was just a facade of course, some scaffolding, sheets of plywood and chipboard, a bit of sawing and painting and there it was. The carpenters were now relaxing at one of the refreshment vans around the car park at Dwejra, bronzed young men with fair hair and baggy shorts that seemed to be weighed down by holsters of saws, hammers and two-way radios.

"Well, Father, you can tell your bosses that they now have a pagan temple instead of a Catholic church," one of them was explaining to Father Jacko. "After the filming, a few hours' work and it will be back to being as Christian as ever." The young man wasn't so much looking at Father Jacko as at the owl sitting on the priest's shoulder. Even with his confident swagger, his gaze retreated before the relentless stare of the owl which, despite its blank expressionless face, seemed to have summed him up and found him wanting.

"That's a barn owl, isn't it?" he ventured. He held his finger out nervously but then reconsidered and withdrew it.

"It's not mine," Jacko hastened to explain. "It belongs to Joseph Zammit. He's gone to get some crisps, from the boathouse."

The chippie shook his head and sniffed. Owls, priests, crisps and boathouses. The whole place was mad. The chances of getting this whole scene filmed with all these lunatics and in the can before the forecast storm hit in a couple of days' time seemed slim. He swallowed a large gulp of lukewarm beer.

"No damage done. Guarantee it. See for yourself, but we're off." With those final remarks, he and his crew jumped into their jeeps and vans. With loud radios blaring and a spinning of wheels, they sped away up the hill.

Father Jacko tickled the owl under its chin, if indeed it had a chin. He was one of the few people the owl would tolerate; maybe because with Jacko's enormous glasses and frequent blank expression, he bore a family resemblance.

After another glass of wine and a chat with various stall-holders Jacko ambled over to the church cum temple and inspected the alterations. He noted that the scaffolding had been secured by a couple of large screws to the tower and reflected that Father Thomas would not like that. Still he wouldn't say anything. He assumed Father Thomas had received a sufficient donation from the film company to ease his conscience at allowing pagan rites and the sacrifice of naked virgins to take place here.

Because tomorrow, with the stunning backdrop of the mighty Azure Window, a famous Italian actress would be led naked across the flat shelf of rock to be chained to a boulder as a sacrificial victim to a sea monster. The scenario had been vividly described by the film's publicists when recruiting a large crowd of extras to form a cheering throng, all dressed, according to the instructions, as ancient Greek peasants.

The word 'naked' had not actually been mentioned, but several of the men claimed to have seen paintings of Andromeda and proclaimed that she was always naked. In countless homes throughout the island, old rugs were being stitched, drapes adapted and shirts cut up. Many maidens, imagining themselves as of classical proportions, were modelling miniscule T-shirts belted at the waist in front of mirrors, and Pietra Azzopardi had reluctantly set aside her latest high heels for a pair of flat sandals, albeit with sparkling hearts on the straps. In countless dreams that night the soft hands of Perseus, rippling like the moonlight on the water, slid sensuously over arched bodies writhing in their chains.

The last of the coaches, tinkling with madonnas, plaster cast Elvises and rosaries, loaded up its tourists and left as the sun began to pale and melt into a garland of violet cloud. Father Jacko climbed down to where a wall of limestone had been sliced neatly into the rock. With his fingers he traced the fossil outlines, creeping in their stratum, embedded and eternal: lizard-like skeletons, spines and curlicues, molluscs and ammonites. Under his feet spread the shattering of mussel shells and sprawling kelp and all the impossible accumulations of petrified life that had made this island while oceans rose and fell and deserts crept, simmered and froze.

By now the sun was layered as yellow as peach against the cliff faces and quiet couples settled into niches of rock, their heads together watching the sun dip into a smudge of red smeared along the rim of the horizon. The blot of the sun sank and purple eruptions of light exploded across the sea and sky. Reverently, awestruck in their shadows, blue in the night, tender as the evening breeze, the young couples rose to go, treading backwards to catch the last embers of sunset as if in deference to some blazing monarch.

Jacko watched it, his heart swimming in love for these people, for the sacredness of this place and the eternity of it. He contemplated the great arch now looming black in the deepening twilight, the shadows creeping into its eroded pillar and fissures and he heard the swell of water beneath it.

The engineers said it would last another hundred years, but from Joseph Zammit's boat the other week Jacko had seen the thinness of the table top and watched the waters circling the spindle of rock that supported it. Joseph assured him it had not changed since he was a child but Owl sat on the bowsprit like a ghostly figurehead nodding as if he had some mysterious foresight. Then he stretched his wings and flew into the evening like some harbinger of doom and made for his perching point on Joseph's refreshment van.

"It won't last," Jacko prophesied one evening, his voice crackling against the rising wind. "Nature made it and Nature will take it away." Silhouetted against the darkening sky, his cassock flapping and his finger pointing, he resembled some ancient sibyl foretelling the apocalypse.

"As long as we make a few lira first," the stall-holders had laughed. "We'll be well inside our tombs before anything happens."

This was how Jacko had found out about the film. A small group of Italians were wandering around the rocks, climbing onto jagged limestone ridges, jumping down into hollows and taking numerous photos of every angle. One of them, watching Jacko's performance, came grinning towards him, a glint of sun on his gold medallion, his gold tooth and his gold cigarette case.

"A crazy, Greek oracle prophesying doom. Would be brilliant. Hadn't thought of it. Complete with owl," he added, as Owl settled onto Jacko's shoulder with his back to the newcomer before revolving his head to fix him with the full force of his indifference.

"What's its name?" the Italian asked, stepping back as Owl flapped his wings and stepped onto Jacko's head, dislodging his glasses.

"Owl," said Joseph, taking the bird back and stroking its ruffled feathers.

"Well, Father," continued the Italian, "how would you and Owl like to feature in a film about Perseus and Andromeda? I can see it now – you racing madly across the top of the arch – distant silhouette against the sky – Owl startling white against the night sky – crazy arms waving, ranting – doom – doom!"

The Italian seemed to be gazing into the far distance of his imagination, his expressive hands drawing the scene in the air – the helpless princess – the cheering crowds – the monster looming up from the turbulent deep.

Jacko, Joseph, Owl and a few bystanders contemplated him doubtfully until they were joined by another of the visitors. From a distance she had seemed lithe and youthful, tripping easily across the rocks with her long hair blowing across her face and shoulders. Closer, the hair was grey, the nose long and pointed and bad temper was etched into the deep wrinkles of her face.

"Marina!" the Italian called. "What about the Father here, and the owl, a mad prophet, oracles, ranting and screaming?"

"I don't think so," she grimaced, her voice flat and scratchy from too many cigarettes. Her small eyes were sunk into deep shadows and she pointed her nose at Jacko like a weapon. "The owl, maybe. We don't want any prophets." And Jacko's possible film career was summarily curtailed.

No one spoke while the Italians exchanged a few observations, gestured at Fungus Rock sleeping on the waves, indicated some other features on the landscape, made notes on clipboards and checked their cameras. Then, without a backward glance, they clambered into a jeep and bumped away up the hill, the sinking sun just catching a last glimmer of gold medallion. Joseph let out a loud guffaw, several of the other men nudged Jacko and Owl pecked a loose strand of his hair.

"There may be no arch there when they come to film it," Jacko muttered.

"You see – no one listens to you and your collapsing arch. It's good for another hundred years," Joseph laughed. "Never mind, Father, I still have some white wine in the ice box. Let us thank God that Hollywood has not stolen Father Jacko away from us."

Father Jacko had avoided crowds and processions ever since the Good Friday incident. The local bands were playing slow music, marching forward a few steps then stopping, marching forward and stopping. Behind them shuffled the hooded penitents dragging massive chains around their ankles. Resplendent on a white horse rode Mario in full Roman armour as he had done every year since his father had retired from the role. Solemnly leading the Pontius Pilate section of the narrative, processed Jacko bearing a sliver cross on a long pole and accompanied by a couple of acolytes wafting incense. Unfortunately, he had misjudged its height as they passed under some decorative lights. Down had come the bare wires wrapping themselves round the Roman soldier whose armour clearly conducted electricity and alarming the splendid white horse which then disposed of its noble rider. From behind there were sparks amongst the chains, a sizzling sound and some yelps as the bare wires increased the penance of the penitents.

When the crowds gathered for the filming, Father Jacko took himself up the hillside with a bag of grapes to witness the spectacle from a safe distance. From early morning the extras had been arriving on trucks, trailers and tractors, donkey carts, cars, rotavators and buses. Film crew were trying to herd the crowds into sections, bellowing through megaphones, confiscating bottles and generally making little impact. Marina, her sharp nose jabbing and harsh voice shouting, was inspecting the costumes. She seemed angry with everyone, pushing some to the back because they were wearing jeans, hauling some out to the front because they looked passable, cursing old men for fumbling, dragging crying children away from their mothers and rapidly becoming the subject of much Gozitan abuse that seemed to need no translation.

A dark-haired girl with a ring in her nose and a pierced eyebrow was writing on a clipboard.

"It's for the credits," she yelled at Joseph. "What's the owl's name?"

"Owl," said Joseph.

Near at hand a dreadful shrieking arose.

"The old bitch has told me to take the hearts off my sandals," Pietra Azzopardi wailed.

"And cover your legs or go to the back," the old bitch commanded, loudly cursing. Marina's T-shirt was wet with sweat and her jeans clung to her slender legs.

Various gantries and staging had been set up for the cameras and thick cables ran hither and thither. Generators spluttered and huge microphones swung from overhead wires.

In the melee sat the director trying to speak into a two-way radio and check his notes. Father Thomas sat beside him in another director's chair, waving imperiously at members of the crew, leaning over to look at the director's notes tapping him on the arm and offering advice. Eventually the director sighed deeply and summoned a young female assistant in halter top and shorts. He whispered something into her ear about a fine Calvados in the director's caravan and the Father seemed eager to be lured away and left the director to direct. Some instructions were given into the two-way radio and the director indicated the high slab of rock that crowned the arch. Immediately Marina cajoled, herded and dragged a straggling convoy of peasants up through the rocks and heat, past the faded and fallen warning signs, and marshalled them in a line along the very crest of the Azure Window.

For a weary hour or so everyone waited. The extras speculated and mumbled.

"I don't see any chains down there," someone whispered.

"She'll be wearing them already," he was expertly answered.

"Naked she'll be. Right in front of us."

"Pity we're not allowed to touch," and a lewd giggle passed through the throng which was already heaving with a mixture of excitement, anticipation and lechery.

"They say they'll strip her cloak off her just as she's passing here," one old man informed his neighbour, rubbing the wizened bristles of his chin.

"Well you won't see anything without your glasses, anyway, you old fool," his wife called out.

Film crew mixing with the crowd began to shush, there was some crackling on the radios and a loud announcement over a megaphone. "Take One."

All eyes went to the plywood temple where an assortment of Greek soldiers in high plumed helmets was dragging out a struggling figure. Her lithesome form wriggled gloriously and a long, slender bare leg peeked out from her robe as she stumbled down the path. On cue, a great cry went up from the crowd, rising and echoing from the cliffs until she came close and beneath the blond wig and torn white cloak there appeared a long-pointed nose, angrily etched wrinkles and a sweaty T-shirt. Suddenly the euphoric cry of the crowd deflated into a huge moan of disappointment and recrimination.

"You didn't think they'd bring the real actress here just for this scene, did you?" a crew member was explaining to a frenzied group of elderly peasants. "They'll use Marina as a stand-in. She's about the same height. They'll dub in the real princess back in the studio."

"Now please sustain the noise this time," the megaphone was announcing. "A cry of eagerness, excitement, exaltation, relief, gratitude! The princess is going to be sacrificed to save you, after all!"

Then, just as the sacrificial victim emerged for the second time, came another announcement, "And there will be as much wine and beer as you can drink when we've finished."

The roar that went up surpassed all expectations. It rattled boulders, echoed from cliff faces and rocked the fishing boats moored down at the inland sea. It woke Father Jacko, clutching his grapes and asleep behind a rock high up beyond the temple. On cue, Owl was let loose and followed by a single camera gracefully flew over the crowd against the backdrop of the Azure Window and then, sighting Jacko, diverted and sailed down upon his bunch of grapes. Jacko, spotting the line of extras ranged along the top of the great arch, was frantically waving his arms and shouting at them to get off before it was too late, it was unsafe, he had seen into the future, it will collapse. It was just at the moment that Owl hit the grapes. Meanwhile the crowd below, awed into silence, witnessed a ranting prophet beating at an owl amid flying feathers and clutching at a bunch of grapes, screaming something apocalyptical, while a panicking throng of Greek peasants fled, slid and rolled down the hillside and a writhing princess pushed aside her escort and started screeching into a two-way radio.

"What do you think you're doing?" the director yelled at Marina over the radio. "The light's fading. We can't afford to do it again."

"We just thought a ranting prophet in the crowd might add something. Didn't anyone tell you? We could put in some entrails; a few auguries perhaps?" she added lamely.

The Director sighed but eventually agreed that with a bit of re-plotting and editing the scene might be rescued.

Jacko discretely allowed the crowds, cameras and crew to disperse before he rather gingerly sneaked out from behind the plywood facade of the temple. Pools of shadow merged with darkness and only the movement of the sea could be heard. He crept down the rough track to the inland sea which lazed in a great hollow of rock behind the boat houses. Little ripples of white crested the shallow water and occasional waves burst through the tunnel that connected it to the Mediterranean beyond, causing the normally placid surface to swell as if the sea itself were breathing in anticipation of the storm to come. Overhead the clouds were spinning swiftly over the moon, making even the meagre moonlight seem nervous.

Jacko wandered over to Joseph's boathouse, felt above the lintel of the door for a key and let himself in. He groped on the window sill for matches and a candle and made himself at home for the night. Among the crates of fizzy drinks and boxes of crisps was an old iron bedstead with a mattress and a blanket and on it Jacko sat, unscrewed a bottle, opened a packet of crisps and settled down to sleep. He could hear the wind siphoning through crevices in the rock and the swish of waves through the tunnel. Beneath his blanket, Jacko prayed for Marina, Joseph Zammit, Father Thomas, Marc, the Englishman he occasionally ran into, and was just entering into intercessions for Owl when he drifted into a turbulent sleep. What was happening outside and what was happening in his dreams mingled, where lightning stabbed the night and thunder rebounded from cliff faces to shattered boulders and crumbling pinnacles of rock. Fossils, dead for eternity reared up and reached out with weedy, spindly tentacles and claws. Vast shelves of timeless stone heaved and split, splintering and tearing like ragged robes and then the sea rose up in a huge explosion of foam and cataract, pounding the tottering pillar of the great sea arch until the massive table top of the Azure Window broke and slid with a grating, crunching rumble and fell into the tempestuous sea.

In the eerie, early morning light Father Jacko locked the door behind him and contemplated the Inland Sea. The boats were still tossing and straining at their moorings and large waves were still funnelling through, but the sky had lightened to a sickly pallor in which a limp disc of sun was faintly visible. Emerging onto the car park which yesterday had been so full of life, Jacko trod round puddles and squelched in his sandals through the clinging grey mud. The pretend temple was a sad ruin of collapsed plywood and scaffolding. Litter blew across the open spaces. Out on the shelf facing the Azure Window were a camera man and a companion with ear phones, a large microphone on a batten and a tape recorder strapped to his belt. Jacko watched them filming great waves rushing in from the open sea and climbing up the pillar that supported the arch until huge surges of water broke, foaming and filling the window before crashing down into the pool below. A great hiss of spray showered over the rocks sending the film team retreating and then tentatively returning to as close to the cliff edge as they dared go. But the Azure Window withstood it all; intact, unyielding, slowly mellowing into the morning sunlight.

"Glad it's still there," the camera man called to Jacko as they packed up to go. "The director particularly wanted those shots."

Contemplating the grizzled, unshaven form before him, he grinned mischievously. "Well, if it isn't our prophet of doom! You've certainly had our editing team working through the night. But you'll have your moment of stardom."

Many months later the little cinema in Victoria was playing to a packed house. The hot, thick darkness was fetid with cigarette smoke, beer and popcorn and there was the sound of excited chatter as the seats filled up. Pietra Azzopardi in the front row with her long, languorous legs stretched in front of her and a Coca Cola to her pouted, ruby lips; Father Thomas, with his church hierarchy embarrassed to be there but in the best seats; in the back row, feet up on the seats in front and their hands rummaging in their popcorn, a mob of loungers, the extras, Father Jacko and Joseph Zammit but no Owl. And about half way down against the wall, Barry.

The crowd scene, for which this gathering had come together in such eager anticipation, lasted less than five minutes. There were some claims from the audience that there was 'so and so', but in general it was an anonymous mob through which a blowing blonde head of hair with an occasional flash of thigh was hustled. Some very loud screams had been dubbed over the baying mob. But Father Jacko, whose eyes were hurting, was dozing in the dark, dreaming of the fossils engraved for millennia into the rock: the lizards and kelp, the ammonites and fragments of mussels patiently bearing the flip-flops of humankind for a moment or two. Sharp nudges from either side brought him back to consciousness and he blinked at the screen.

The lovely victim stood chained to her polystyrene rock disappointingly well covered but nevertheless enticingly wet. She struggled and shrieked alluringly but the rock wasn't Dwerja and the audience grumbled loudly. Then came some shots of huge surges of foam and water, of crashing waves and spray guttering through the mighty rock window, and out of it, rising from the sea, a great rubbery monster grimacing and pounding the roof of the arch, hungry for the maiden's flesh.

Then followed the cheers, applause and laughter. Fleeing from the creature, tumbling and sliding, trampling each other, rolling down slopes, clambering over rocks, in panic, the out of control crowds were chased from the top of the arch. And silhouetted black against the sky, buffeted by a crazed and ominous owl, the prophet, ranting and raving doom, urged them on, dragging them and pushing them from the fragile shelf of the window top. It was all over in ten seconds.

Joseph Zammit and Owl, Pietra, Eddie, Mrs Vella and all the extras sat at their tables in the warm night, drank beer and lamented the perfidy of virgin princesses and sea monsters. Among the tables, slowly, smiling, walked Father Jacko. He patted Joseph on the shoulder and shared a joke. "It will happen. It will happen," he warned. He made the sign of the cross over Pietra feeding her baby from a bottle as she sat with her mother, grandmother, Eddie and Mrs Vella. Finally, he passed Barry sipping a quiet beer in the shadows, paused and blessed him, then silently disappeared into the night.

The new century would come with tourist coaches in ever increasing numbers and apartments would jostle for views along the sheer ridges; the currency would change and even the Azure Window would one day pivot on its storm-stressed pillar and fall. Father Jacko would run waving his arms among the crowd for as long as celluloid lasts, but the fossilised fauna of the sea would be the island for eternity.

Lightning Source UK Ltd.
Milton Keynes UK
UKHW020655170822
407432UK00011B/1757